I0607717

THE HEIR

The Amulet Saga
Volume One

by

Avily Jerome

THE HEIR
Published by Dragontail Press
P. O. Box 54550
Phoenix, AZ 85078

ISBN 978-1-7321879-3-1
Copyright © 2015 by Avily Jerome
Cover art concept by Sarah Collotta
Cover design by Kirk DouPonce, Dog Eared Design

Available in print from your local bookstore, online, or from the author at:
www.avilyjerome.com

For more information on this book and the author visit: www.avilyjerome.com

All rights reserved. Non-commercial interests may reproduce portions of this book without the express written permission of the author, provided the text does not exceed 500 words. When reproducing text from this book, include the following credit line: *"The Amulet Saga, Volume One: The Heir* by Avily Jerome, published by **Dragontail Press. For more information visit www.avilyjerome.com. Used by permission."**

Commercial interests: No part of this publication may be reproduced in any form, stored in a retrieval system, or transmitted in any form by any means—electronic, photocopy, recording, or otherwise—without prior written permission of the author, except as provided by the United States of America copyright law.

This is a work of fiction. Names, characters, and incidents are all products of the author's imagination or are used for fictional purposes. Any mentioned brand names, places, and trademarks remain the property of their respective owners, bear no association with the author or the publisher, and are used for fictional purposes only.

Brought to you by Avily Jerome

Library of Congress Cataloging-in-Publication Data
Jerome, Avily
The Heir/Avily Jerome 1st ed.

Printed in the United States of America.

Praise for *The Heir*
and for Avily Jerome

"Avily loves story. I'm delighted she now has the chance in *The Heir* to share her love with the world."

— **Kerry Nietz, author of *Amish Vampires in Space***

"*The Amulet Saga* is a great introduction to Avily Jerome's fantastical adventures. Magical creatures, treacherous royals, a nation in peril, and a healthy splash of romance—what's not to love?"

— **Lindsay Franklin, author and editor**

"Avily Jerome is a brilliant storyteller. *The Amulet Saga* is classic fantasy at its finest. You'll be drawn in to this world and never want to leave."

— **Ben Wolf, author of *Blood for Blood***

"*The Heir* is a great fantasy tale complete with magical creatures, an inescapable forest, and an assassin whose primary target is sorcerers. Avily Jerome weaves a beautiful tale of heroism, courage, and self-sacrifice in this first installment of The Amulet Saga. I definitely want to know what happens next."

— **S. D. Grimm, author of *The Children of the Blood Moon***

"Avily Jerome can transport a reader to a worlds unknown in only a few well-crafted sentences. Her stories are worth savoring to catch every little moment."

— **Lindsey Brackett, Web Content Editor for Splickety Publishing Group and Community Columnist**

For my husband, the man who supports my writing habits and puts up with all my quirks. I love you.

Acknowledgments

Special thanks to my mom, who taught me to read and instilled a love of literature in me, who always encouraged me, and who made sure I could write coherent sentences.

Thanks to my husband, who supports me financially and emotionally, and who allows me to pursue my passion.

Thanks also to Lindsay Franklin, who edited this story and helped me brainstorm.

I'd like to add a nod to The New Authors Fellowship Blog, (www.newauthors.wordpress.com) where I was a contributing blogger for several years and where this story was born.

And, of course, thank you to my readers, the ones who waited weekly for the next installment of this series on the blog and who continue to come back for more.

The daughter of the dragon
Who oversees the land
Will live until the day
The dragons come again

Love she'll never know
A child she'll never have
The kings and queens of fate
Her legacy will show

From the path fate strays
The Lover and the Traitor
When the Solstice Moon shines brightly
And at the Dragon, the Dancer waves

Across the ocean wide
The darkness rises swiftly
Untold power unleashed
Building until that day

The reign of power shifts
Fate in the balance
The weight of choices made
Brings life or the end of all

The child lost arises
To take the power back
A child of the enemy
Begotten then to conquer

When the dragons rise again
When the mountains open wide
When the stones of heaven fall
The world is remade.

When the darkness reigns
Then the hate shall bind
The hearts of one and all
Until the light is found

Those who triumph fall
Those who seek shall find
Those who rule shall serve
The servant, ruler of all

The begotten of the dragons
Beloved of the Creator
Who bears the Dragon Stone
The Deliverer of the World

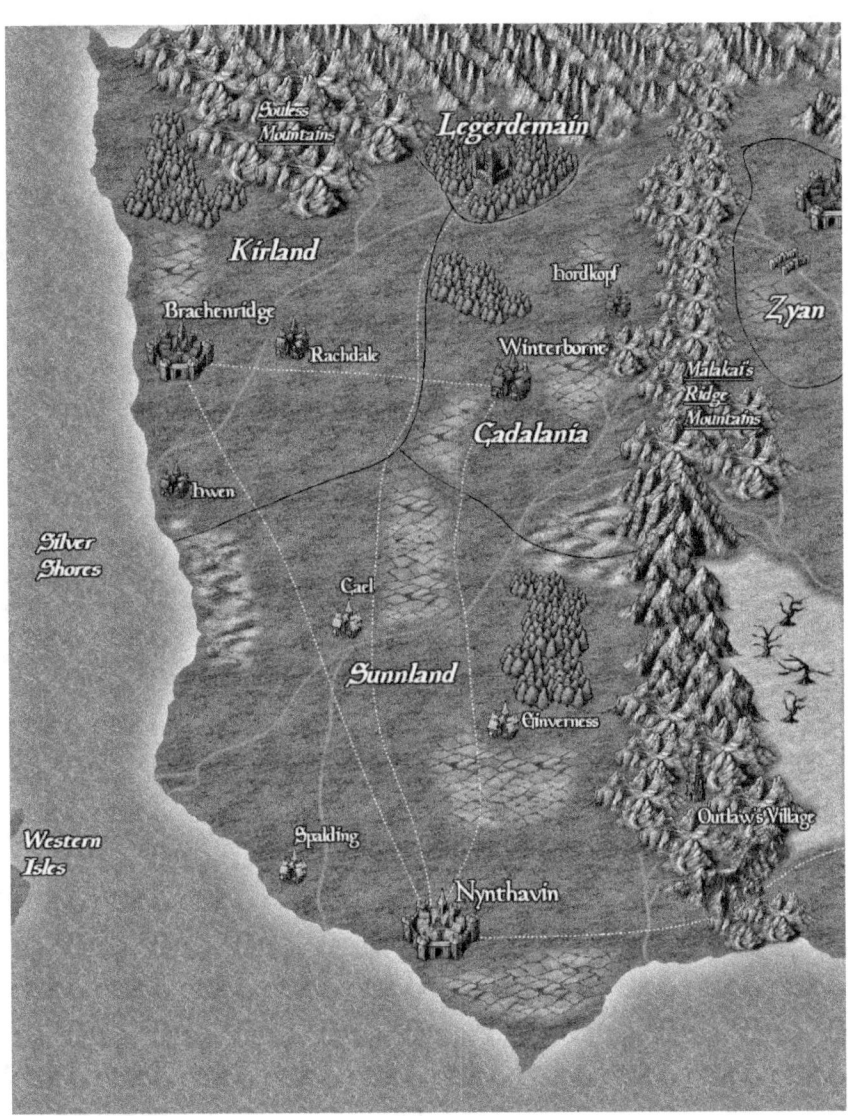

Souless
Mountains

Legerdemain

Kirland

hordkopf

Zyan

Brachenridge

Rachdale

Winterborne

Malakai's
Ridge
Mountains

Çadalania

Ihwen

Silver
Shores

Cael

Sunnland

Ginverness

Western
Isles

Spalding

Outlaw's Village

Nynthavin

Table of Contents

Rendezvous

Rina crept toward her spy's body.

She shouldn't have let him go. She should have stopped him, somehow.

Using the trees for cover, her feet soundless on the wet leaves covering the ground, she took another step.

Whoever killed him must know he'd intended to meet her, and that meant they were probably close. She had to get to him before they did.

His horse stood near his body. It whickered and looked back along the path it travelled before its rider fell.

Rina pulled a knife from the collection she wore strapped to her belt before continuing.

She didn't see anyone approaching.

The spy carried a bulging satchel over his shoulder. What he'd gone to steal must be in there.

She took another step.

The crack of a twig coming from behind the horse stopped her. She peeked from behind the protection of a tree, scanning for movement.

A moment later, a crouched, hobbling figure crept out of the brush to the side of the path and approached the body.

A woman?

Gnarled fingers reached up and pulled back the hood of her cloak to reveal an aged face framed by wispy silver hair. Her eyes darted around, scanning the clearing.

What was this crone doing out here? Did she not know the terrors that lurked in these woods? She must want the satchel as badly as Rina. All the more reason for Rina to get it first.

Rina threw her knife. It landed with a *thunk* in a tree, inches from the woman's head.

The woman whimpered, standing still and lifting her hands in the air. "Please don't kill me. He stole something from me. Let me take it, and you can have any other valuables you find on him."

Rina remained hidden. "Leave this place at once. You may take the horse, but you must go. If you stay, I cannot guarantee your safety."

The old woman gave a shaky laugh and took another step forward. "If I do not get back what he stole, I will die anyway."

"What he has is mine."

The woman bowed her head. "I can see the future. If you let me leave with what is mine, I will tell your fortune."

The hag took another step. Rina threw another knife, this one landing near the woman's feet.

"Please," the woman begged. "My people are in danger. The king is in danger."

"The king is evil. If what's in that bag helps you save him, you give me another reason to stop you." Rina drew another knife. A pang shot through her. It was the knife he'd given her.

"You don't understand." The woman's voice cracked. "I have seen the future. The one who kills the king will destroy us all."

"Perhaps death is better than life under a king who oppresses his people and forces his magicians to fill the woods with monsters so none can escape his rule."

"You escaped."

"I did. And I will help others, using what is in that bag."

"I cannot let you have it." The old woman dropped her arms and made a dash for the body.

Rina threw again. The knife struck the hag in the chest.

The old woman collapsed, writhing, her fingers still grasping at the satchel.

Rina emerged from her hiding place. She paused just a moment to say a prayer over her spy's body before she picked up the satchel and opened it. Inside was the amulet.

"With this, I can break the king's protection so he can be killed. Why would you not want me to have it?"

The wizened eyes stared up at her, wide with horror. "It's you. You're the one who will kill us all."

The Amulet

Twenty Years Earlier

"I regret being the one to tell you this, but your father is gone."

William stared at his old nurse, hardly comprehending. "Gone?"

"I'm so sorry, my dear boy." The old woman, Ada, held open her arms to him.

Part of him wanted to go to her, to find comfort in her embrace, as he had from the moment of his birth, but he stiffened and took a step back.

"It's my half-brother, isn't it?"

"No one is certain what happened. You know his heart has been ailing him."

"Don't lie to spare my feelings. Maury has always wanted the throne. And now that my father is gone, he'll have no trouble wresting control away from me."

The woman's eyes looked pained. She seemed older than usual. William couldn't remember her ever looking anything other than ancient, but the creases that accented her features seemed particularly deep today.

He forced himself to see beyond the façade of caring nurse to what she really was—a co-conspirator with his half-brother for the throne. The throne that rightfully belonged to him.

Shoving past, he stalked down the hall toward his father's chamber.

Maury sat at the foot of the bed, his shoulders slumped, his face drawn in an expression affecting sorrow at the king's passing. He looked up when William entered. "What are you doing here?"

"I'm paying my respects to *my* father."

Maury nodded, but his eyes went to the guard that stood by the

13

door.

William seethed. As if he would desecrate his father's deathbed by picking a fight here, now.

He took his father's lifeless hand and held it, feeling the cold flesh slide over the bones. The king's lips looked blue around the edges, and his face had a sickly pallor. That the death was unnatural seemed obvious to William, but he had no proof. Not yet. He would demand that tests and enchantments were performed, and he would find out the truth.

He turned to Maury, plastering a smile on his face. "Thank you for your attention to him, brother. I know I can count on your continued support at my coronation."

Maury's face paled; his jaw formed a hard line. "*Your* coronation?"

"Of course. I am the king's son. The royal line falls to me."

"*Our* mother was the queen before she married him. The royal line follows blood, and I am the firstborn."

"Parliament will agree that, as I am the son of both nobles and no one knows the identity of your father, I am the rightful heir," William insisted.

"We shall discuss it at the council tomorrow," Maury said in that superior tone he always used to assert his authority as the eldest.

William narrowed his eyes. "Yes. Tomorrow."

William returned to his room. Spending time in seclusion to mourn would not be looked on with suspicion.

His knowledge of enchantments was slim, but he knew enough from watching Ada work to concoct a solution to meet his needs.

He waited until the clock chimed the hour past midnight, then crept out of his room and down the long hallway to his father's chamber. The burial process wouldn't start until the following morning, so he had just enough time to find it.

The guard at the door shifted as though trying to stay awake.

Clearly, he didn't take his duty too seriously, and rightly so. Fear of spirits kept any sane person out of the same room with a corpse the night after a death.

William crept on silent feet toward the guard, keeping to the shadows, and pulled out the concoction-doused handkerchief from his bag.

Holding his breath, so not to breathe the foul smell himself, he sprang toward the guard and placed the handkerchief under his nose.

The guard stepped back in surprise, but within moments slumped to the floor.

William stepped over him and slid into the room. He made his way to his father's body. A chill ran through him, like a cold breeze passing, only the window was tightly shuttered. He hoped his father's spirit knew his intentions were pure as he reached his hands toward the king's neck and pulled away the chain that hung against his chest.

The next morning, he held his head high at the meeting of the council.

He scarcely had time to sit before the Grand Vizier stood and held out his hands for silence. "It pains me, in this time of tragedy, to have to perform such a duty, but the country must not be without a king. And so it is with both joy and reluctance that I name the firstborn son of Her Majesty, Queen Rose of the royal line of Legerdemain, Maury, King of Legerdemain, Ruler of the Four Villages, and Ambassador to the Outer Nations."

William jumped from his chair. "This is preposterous. I am the rightful heir."

The Grand Vizier held up his hand. "I understand your frustration, William, but the council has discussed it in depth, and we agree that as the firstborn son of your mother, Maury is the rightful king."

"If my father wanted the crown to be passed to Maury, why did

15

he give this to me?" William held up his hand. Around his fingers dangled a gold chain, from which hung a brilliant purple stone set in an ornate amulet with writing from the Old Language etched in it.

A gasp rose from the rest of the people sitting at the table.

"I don't know why your father would give you that, but it was not his to give. It belongs to the royal line, and now it belongs to Maury."

"No. My father gave it to me."

"You will relinquish it before your brother's coronation next week. That is all."

The Grand Vizier made a spectacular exit, his robes flowing behind him and the rest of the council trailing after.

William stood alone in the room and clutched the jewel. Maury might take the crown, but he would never get the amulet.

Sorcerer

"I heard you were looking for a sorcerer."

The man at the rough, wooden table looked up. "I am. Please sit."

Jarok sat, but kept the hood of his cloak up to shade his face from prying eyes.

A wench set a mug of ale before him.

He waited until she was out of earshot and faced the man he'd come to meet. "What sort of magics do you wish performed?"

"I need a way to keep the people from leaving the country. I wish them to stay, but already the threat of civil war has incited many to leave their homes and emigrate to other kingdoms."

Jarok stared at the stranger. "What business is it of yours whether people choose to stay or go?"

"Very soon I will be king, and I wish to still have a kingdom when I take the throne."

"I see. And what would be the terms of my employment?"

"You would stay here, in this kingdom, as one of my citizens, ready to do as I bid, but you would be free to live your life and do as you like when I do not have need of you. Name your price for your wages. When I am king, you will have it."

Jarok considered the offer. He could do far worse. In many parts of the world, sorcerers were hunted and despised. To live in peace, to practice his art without fear of reprisal, that was a temptation not to be considered lightly.

Of course, working for free was not ideal, even if it was temporary. His payment would be entirely dependent on his success.

Perhaps that's what the man was counting on.

At any rate, he'd lived on worse. "Very well. You may consider me hired. What do you have in mind as a way to keep your citizens contained?"

"I know little of magic. I thought perhaps a barrier of some kind that people could not pass through would be appropriate."

Jarok shook his head. "That would not work. A spell of that scale would take far more magic than a dozen sorcerers could conjure, let alone maintain. Moreover, unless you want to close everyone off from the outside world, trade and commerce included, a barrier is not the sort of device you want. I noticed as I came to town that the road goes through a dense forest. How far does the forest extend?"

"It encircles the entire kingdom."

Jarok nodded. "How many roads in and out?"

"Just one, the one you came in on."

"Good. I know what to do. I have a particular gift for conjuring animals. I can create a beast that will roam the forest and devour anyone who tries to leave. Then you can put guards on the road to prevent anyone without authorization to leave."

"What is to keep a beast from coming into the villages to devour my people, or wandering away completely?"

"I will put a spell on it that prevents it from leaving the forest, even to go on the road."

"How will one beast keep the entire forest safe from people trying to leave?"

"I can make more than one. We will fill the forest with creatures that will hunt down any human that enters it."

"What will keep people from killing the beasts?"

Jarok smiled. "Magical creatures have few weaknesses. These beasts will have protection that renders weapons useless and an insatiable hunger for human flesh that will cause them to seek out any person who enters their territory."

The stranger rubbed his hands together. "Yes, that will do. One thing concerns me, however. You said the creature will have *few* weaknesses. That means it can be killed, if the weakness is found."

"Yes."

"Can you not make it invulnerable?"

"All magic has limits. All spells can be broken. However, the chance that anyone could find the weakness before he is killed is slim."

The stranger nodded. "Very well. Let us begin at once. What do you need?"

"I need a space to work, preferably near the forest's entrance so I can release the creatures as soon as I create them. I will need you to trap animals, live ones, for me to work with. I cannot create something out of nothing, but I can change what already exists. And I will need help. Such a task will require more strength than I have alone. Is there anyone in your kingdom with magic?"

The stranger shook his head. "Only one old woman who works in the palace, and her magic is limited to a few potions and vague predictions."

"Then you will need to hire more from outside."

The stranger nodded. "I will see to it immediately."

"Good. Then I need one more thing from you. I need some sort of charm, something powerful that will channel the magic and bind the creatures to you. The spell will connect you to the creatures, giving you their strength and invulnerability, and giving you power over them. You will be able to control them and kill them, but if something should happen to you, the creatures will lose their power and become vulnerable."

"What sort of thing do you need?"

"It can be anything. Something that belongs to you but has inherent value, and if possible, something that is magical on its own."

The stranger pulled a heavy gold chain from his neck and set it on the table between them. A gold pendant, set with a brilliant purple

19

stone and inscribed with letters of the Old Language, hung from the chain.

Jarok reached for it. The magic in him vibrated against the aura that emanated from the amulet, making his ears ring. The necklace held a very old, very powerful magic. He picked it up and felt the depth of its power. "Where did you get this?"

"It is mine," the stranger snapped. "It was given to me by my father, passed down from my mother's line for generations."

Jarok held it in his hands and repeated a simple incantation. He looked up at the stranger. "It is not yours. Not wholly, anyway."

The stranger's eyes narrowed. "It *is* mine."

Jarok held his gaze. "I have no care for who rules this country. I care only for my wages. This holds powerful magic, and it is more than ideal for completing my spell, but it must be yours. There is another with equal rights to it. You must convince him to relinquish his rights, and the agreement must be in blood. The other's blood on the amulet will seal the bargain. Can you do this?"

The stranger nodded. "I can convince him."

"Good," Jarok said. "Then I will meet you here tomorrow and we can begin our work."

Blood Ties

"It is not yours. Not wholly, anyway." The sorcerer's eyes held suspicion, distrust.

William took the amulet back from the sorcerer, tracing the gold letters etched in its casing with his fingers. What did it mean? What magic had been stored there so long ago? Even the sorcerer seemed surprised by the depth of its power. Not that the amulet's original purpose mattered, so many hundreds of years later. What mattered now was the power he would give to it—and get from it in return.

He looked across the table at the sorcerer. It had shocked him, when the sorcerer's hood fell back, revealing his face, how young he appeared. Scarcely older than William. Of course, an older, more experienced sorcerer probably wouldn't have agreed to work on a promise. William would take what fate handed him. But this sorcerer had better come through with his end of the bargain.

The sorcerer held William's gaze. "I have no care for who rules this country. I care only for my wages. This holds powerful magic, and it is more than ideal for completing my spell, but it must be yours. There is another with equal rights to it. You must convince him to relinquish his rights, and the agreement must be in blood. The other's blood on the amulet will seal the bargain. Can you do this?"

William nodded. "I can convince him."

He'd fled the palace before Maury's coronation. Parliament would've forced him to give up the amulet, otherwise. He'd been living in hovels around the Four Villages since then, planning just how he'd take back what was rightfully his.

And now he had a way.

Keeping the amulet had been necessary, he knew that all along. Now, he just had to determine what would be the most efficient way to convince Maury to relinquish any claim on it.

He gazed into amethyst. In his mind, he saw Maury's wife, the queen, her face pale, brow covered in a sheen of sweat, as she'd been the last time he'd seen her. Ada had insisted the queen stay in bed for the duration of her pregnancy after a fall had caused contractions early on.

The more he thought about it, the more convinced William was that using the queen was his best chance to convince Maury.

"I need a potion. Something that will ensure the safe delivery of a baby. Can you make something like that?"

The sorcerer nodded.

"How long will it take?"

"A few hours, with the right supplies."

"Tell me what you need and I'll get it for you. Let me know when it's ready. The amulet will be mine by sundown."

"Good," the sorcerer said. "Then I will meet you here tomorrow and we can begin our work on the creature."

After acquiring the supplies for the potion, William wrote a note to his brother the king and sent it with a messenger to the palace.

There was a shop in the South Village that sold herbs and other ingredients, including the sorts of rare items needed for potions. William had taken enough gold with him from the castle to purchase what he needed without difficulty. He shrouded himself in a cloak whenever he walked through the villages, to minimize the chances of being recognized. He purchased what he needed and met the sorcerer in the small, uninhabited cottage he'd been using near the edge of the forest.

The sorcerer had already started a fire in the fireplace and had an array of jars and bowls spread out on the table. William handed him the ingredients.

The sorcerer muttered to himself while he carefully measured the herbs and mixed them in the bowls, heated them, tested them, and mixed some more. At last, he poured the final potion into a small vial and sealed it with a cork.

"Be careful with that."

The sorcerer then taught him an incantation, having him repeat it carefully, so every word, every syllable was exact. William didn't understand the Old words, but he repeated them precisely.

This spell had to be exact.

The sun would set soon. Maury would be coming. William made his way to the edge of the woods to wait.

Before long, Maury strode toward him.

A cold wind whipped through the field that bordered the forest. William pulled his cloak a little tighter, ignoring the sense of foreboding that accompanied it. "Hello, Maury."

"William. You have the potion?"

"Of course."

"What do you want? You said you needed something from me."

"The amulet."

Maury crossed his arms in front of his chest. "You already took the amulet."

"Yes. But I need you to relinquish your rights to it."

"How? Why?"

"The why is of no importance. The how involves your oath that you relinquish the amulet to me, sealed by your blood on the Old words."

"And in exchange you'll give me the potion? You can guarantee she'll be safe? The baby will be safe?"

William smiled. "You have my word."

"I'll do it."

"You understand the terms of the deal?"

"Yes! I already said yes. What do I do?"

William extended a knife with a jeweled hilt. "Your blood."

Maury sliced the palm of his hand. He didn't even wince.

William held out the amulet and spoke the words the sorcerer had instructed, while Maury squeezed his blood onto the etchings in the gold that encased the jewel.

"Your oath."

"I swear on my life and my blood to relinquish all claim to the amulet of my ancestors. It is no longer mine, but belongs solely to my brother, William."

William caught movement at the edge of the trees. He glanced up and saw a figure peering at them from behind a bush.

His old nurse. He smiled. She didn't matter. It was too late. The deal was done.

He handed Maury the potion. "Thank you, brother. It was good to see you. Give my love to your wife and son."

Maury clutched the potion to his chest and fled back toward the palace.

Once Maury was out of sight, he emerged from the shadows and pushed the hood back from his face.

The old woman's face went white when she saw him. She collapsed to the ground. "*You.*"

He smiled. "Hello, Ada. It has been a long time."

"What have you done?" she demanded.

William smiled. "I only took back what is rightfully mine."

He left Ada there, staring after him. The old woman had some remarkable gifts, but clearly she hadn't seen this coming.

Good.

It wouldn't be the last surprise to come her way.

***

The sorcerer was gone by the time William returned to the cottage. He secured the amulet around his neck and tucked it safely beneath his shirt, where he could feel its warmth radiating against his skin.

It was well and truly his, now. Even if Maury somehow managed to steal it back, the magic was bound to William alone.

He banked the fire and pulled his cloak around him for a blanket. The first thing he would do when he was king would be burn this disgusting shack.

The sorcerer returned the next morning, just as the sun began to peek through the cracks in the walls.

"Do you have it?"

William handed him the amulet.

The sorcerer's features darkened.

"What is it? Can't you do the spell?"

The sorcerer looked up. "Oh, I can do the spell. This will work nicely for that. It's just…the magic in this amulet. It's older and more powerful than I dreamed."

"Isn't that good? Won't more power help us?"

"Yes, if you can control it."

"What do you mean 'if'? Isn't that why I made my brother swear the oath with his blood?"

"That was enough to claim the amulet for yourself. For now. But the magic is linked inextricably to blood. It is yours now, but any heir to the blood can claim it."

"You're saying even though Maury relinquished the amulet to me, he or one of his children can still claim it."

"Yes."

William nodded. "Then I'll make sure Maury doesn't leave an heir."

The Storm

Ada gazed into the bowl. An image shimmered in the water, just out of focus.

25

Something was coming. Something dire.

She spoke all the enchantments she knew, yet the bowl would not reveal the future with any clarity.

At length, she stood, bones creaking and joints popping, and covered the bowl with a cloth. Her duties called.

She blew out the single candle, bathing the room in thick darkness.

The heavy oak door squeaked when she pulled it open, and dim light from the torches that lined the hallway illuminated her way. The slap of her sandals on the stone echoed down the long corridor as she made her way to the narrow stairs that led to the main level of the palace.

"Hurry, Ada, the queen is stirring," one of the maids urged, taking her arm to help her up the last few stairs.

Ada shuffled to the queen's chamber and sat by the bed.

She sprinkled a variety of herbs into the cup of water on the bedside table, then put the concoction to the queen's lips.

The queen sputtered, coughing up half of what Ada poured down her throat, but Ada persisted.

"How is she?"

Ada turned toward the voice. "No worse today, I think, Your Majesty."

The king nodded, the concern on his face softening. "And the baby?"

She pressed her hands to the queen's abdomen. "He still lives, but he is weak."

The king stepped closer and brushed the queen's face with his fingertips. "If there's anything I can do…"

Ada patted his arm. "I know. We all feel that way. I'm doing everything I can."

Someone tapped at the door.

Ada turned to the servant who stood nearby. "Tell whoever that is to leave. The queen needs her rest."

The servant hurried out into the hall. Hushed voices echoed over the stone walls, and the servant returned a moment later.

She curtsied before the king. "Urgent message for you, Your Majesty."

The king turned and swept from the room.

Ada finished feeding herbs to the queen, then prepared another batch for the queen's attendant to administer later. She softly sang a prayer as she worked.

The queen's breathing slowed to the rhythmic cadence of peaceful sleep.

Ada crept from the room and made her way to the stable. "Good morning, James," she said to the stable master. "Have Rosebud saddled for me, please."

James snapped his fingers at the stable boy who hovered nearby, then turned back to Ada. "You're going out today? Are you sure that's wise? A storm is coming."

"I'm almost out of herbs, and the queen's health depends on them."

"You need a new apprentice."

Ada chuckled. "That I do. Let me know if you find one that won't turn out the same as the last one."

The stable boy reappeared then, leading Ada's docile mare. Ada bid James farewell.

The sun was already beginning its descent by the time she reached the glade at the edge of the forest where the highest concentration of herbs could be found.

She left Rosebud next to a tree and made her way down the bank to the edge of the stream and began selecting herbs and placing them in her basket.

A breeze whistled by her, ruffling her hair. She stood and sniffed the air. Something in the wind reminded her of the half-formed vision she'd seen in the bowl that morning, hinting at some impending menace approaching.

A shiver ran up her spine, but she pushed the sensation away. The queen's health was a more immediate concern.

She wandered further, closer to the edge of the forest, searching out the most potent herbs.

A noise caught her attention and she paused, listening for the source of the sound.

She saw the flap of a cloak waving in the breeze, just inside the tree line, and crept closer. Two men stood in the shadows, one wearing the cloak she'd seen, the other wearing all black, his face concealed by a low hat.

"You understand the terms of the deal?" a low, sinister voice asked.

The man in the hat nodded.

"Good," the cloaked man said. "Seal it." He extended a knife with a jeweled hilt, then held out his gloved hand. Something he held caught the sun, and a beam of amethyst light blinded Ada for a moment.

The man in the hat took the knife and sliced the palm of his hand with it, letting the blood drip onto the thing in the other man's hand.

The cloaked man's hand clenched around whatever it was he held, and he laughed, a low, haunting laugh that carried on the wind and chilled Ada to her bones.

The man in the hat returned the knife, then whirled around.

Ada stifled a gasp.

The king.

What was he doing here? And what sort of deal had he just made?

The cloaked man turned slightly toward Ada. She shrank back

further into the bushes to avoid being seen.

The king hurried away without ever noticing Ada.

Not so with the man in the cloak.

He emerged from the shadows and pushed the hood back from his face.

The strength left Ada's limbs, and she collapsed to the ground. "*You.*"

He smiled. "Hello, Ada. It has been a long time."

"What have you done?" she demanded.

He just smiled. "I only took back what is rightfully mine."

He turned and disappeared into the forest.

A gust of wind whipped around Ada, and dark clouds covered the sun. A storm was indeed coming.

Creature

"I just got a report of another attack, Your Majesty."

Maury turned toward the messenger who brought the news. "Like the others?"

"Yes."

"And the hunters?"

"The hunting party is still out, but the last report said they lost the creature in the woods."

"Keep me informed."

The messenger bowed and left the room. Maury turned to the old woman who sat on the chair to the right of the throne. "Any insights, Ada?"

"The creature is not natural, that much I know. Magic was involved in its creation. Magic stronger and more powerful than any I can claim."

"Can it be stopped?"

"All magic can be stopped, and all creatures can be killed, but beyond those basic truths, I have no answers for you."

Maury paced the dais. "Where did it come from?"

"My king, you know the answer to that without any assistance from my seeing."

Maury stopped at the window and stared out at the seemingly endless forest that encircled his kingdom. The forest that started as a grove over a thousand years before, meant to protect the kingdom from attackers, was now home to the very things that threatened to destroy the kingdom and everything in it.

"William."

"Yes," the old woman confirmed.

"What does he want?"

30

"That, too, is a question to which you already know the answer."

"The throne. He still believes he is the rightful heir."

Far away, so far that they looked like a swarm of insects, a flock of black birds rose above the trees in a flurry of panicked flight.

"What can he hope to accomplish by this?"

"He is holding the kingdom hostage. Your people will rebel if they believe you cannot keep them safe. When they are rioting, demanding that you protect them even though you cannot, then William will come to claim the throne with the promise that he will rid the kingdom of the very creatures he brought forth."

"You can see all that with your enchantments?"

"No. I have known your brother since his birth. It does not require magic to understand his methods. He will continue to increase his power in order to turn the people against you. He will kill them until you no longer have a kingdom to rule."

"Then I have no choice but to surrender the kingdom to him."

"I wouldn't say that. If you want to keep your people safe, you must find a way to destroy the creature."

Maury continued to gaze at the forest, but he no longer really saw it. How could he kill a magical creature, when the only magic he'd ever possessed, he'd forfeited to his brother? But how could he regret saving the life of his wife and unborn son?

He glanced at Ada. So frail, yet the source of so much wisdom and strength. "Tell me what to do."

She bowed her head. "I will do all in my power to find a solution."

***

Before dawn the next morning, Maury was awakened by commotion in the hallway outside his chambers.

He glanced at his wife, sleeping fitfully beside him, and rolled from the bed to find the source of the racket. Her pregnancy was not

31

going well, despite the potion, and he didn't want her to lose any more rest.

He threw on a robe and went out into the hallway. "What's going on?"

"Your Majesty, the hunting party has returned. What's left of it."

"What do you mean?"

A man stepped forward. His clothes were torn and bloody, and the side of his face was blackened, the flesh seared.

Maury sucked in his breath. "What—"

"We found the creature's lair." The hunter's voice rasped, scarcely audible. "It was like nothing I've ever seen before. All my men—everyone except for me—"

The hunter collapsed, his armor clattering against the marble floor.

"Get Ada. Quickly," Maury ordered.

The guard disappeared, and Maury bent toward the hunter. "Can you tell me how to reach the creature's lair?"

Just as the hunter finished giving Maury instructions, Ada appeared and began her ministrations on the wounded man.

Maury turned to the guard. "Gather the army. We're going after the creature. And send servants to take care of this man."

Within moments, the hall buzzed with activity. Ada barked orders at the servants, instructing them in caring for the man. When all was quiet, she addressed Maury. "I'm going with you."

"No, I can't risk you getting hurt."

"How many of your men have already died? This creature is magical. Our best chance of killing it is with magic, and I am the only one who knows any. Perhaps I can figure out its weaknesses. Or at least what it is and how it was conjured."

"What about the queen? If something happens to you, who will care for her? And my son, my heir, who grows inside her. Who will

32

keep him safe?"

The old woman nodded. "I understand your concern, but if we do not destroy the creature, there will be no kingdom left for him to inherit. I am coming."

Maury sighed, but nodded. "I'll have your horse saddled."

***

The forest was dark, the early morning sun scarcely penetrating the thick canopy.

Maury led his army, a single-file line, deeper into the trees, following the hunter's directions.

The silence grew as thick as the trees the further they went. The air felt heavy, closing in around them. Even the horses seemed subdued as they dutifully followed their riders' commands.

"We should be close," Maury whispered.

A moment later, they entered a small clearing.

Bits of armor and broken weapons littered the trampled grass, but there was no sign of the slain bodies of the hunting party.

A chill ran through Maury, making the hair on the back of his neck stand on end.

At the opposite end of the clearing, in a small burrow that looked almost like a cave in the underbrush, a pair of amethyst eyes glowed.

Maury drew his sword. "Get ready, men!"

A head like a dragon attached to the body of a lion with the wings and claws of an eagle emerged from the hole, which seemed far too small, and filled the clearing. It raised itself up on its hind legs, its claws digging into the earth, its front talons pawing the air above Maury's head.

The creature hissed and opened its mouth.

Maury raised his sword and shield, dug his heels into his horse's sides, and charged.

A burst of flame washed over him, heating the metal of his armor

33

so it burned him. Blisters opened on his arms. Blood trickled down over his hands, the hilt of his sword, onto its blade. He pushed on, rushing toward the thing, thrusting his sword upward.

The beast screeched and drew back.

Black blood seeped from its chest.

The army rushed in, closing on the beast.

It swiveled, snapping its jaws at the nearest soldier, snatching him from his horse, devouring him even as it swiped at another soldier with its front talons.

One after another, the beast killed Maury's men, not seeming to tire.

Maury couldn't understand it. Why were they unable to kill it, after he'd wounded it?

Ada's voice filled the clearing. "Stop!"

The sound held a hypnotic note that compelled even the beast to pause; for a moment, the whole forest stood still.

Ada looked at Maury. "You must kill it, Your Majesty. Only you can."

Maury rushed forward, swinging his sword at the monster's neck.

The sun reflected in the creature's eyes, a flash of violet, just before they shifted to a dull, dead black as the creature's head separated from its body.

Time resumed its flow, and the army surged in to surround the king.

"Bring the body," Ada ordered. "I need to study it." She turned her horse toward home.

Maury rode to catch up. "Why the hurry? It's dead. We're safe."

"Don't be a fool. That wasn't the only one of its kind. We are nowhere near safe."

"That's why you want to study it."

Ada nodded.

They rode in silence for a moment before Maury spoke again. "How did you know I could kill it?"

"I smelled it in the wind."

"Why was I able to kill it when my men weren't?"

Ada looked at him, her eyes seeming to read his very soul. "When I can answer that, then we will be safe."

Premonition

Jarok showed the three newest sorcerers how to complete the incantation over the cougar he'd captured. He'd already mixed the potion and applied it, and now the three sorcerers held the amulet as they chanted the words to transform the beast into a monster. The mixture of forest plants in the potion would confine the creature to the woods, while the power from the amulet would protect William and allow him to control the creatures.

William stood in the corner of the room, arms crossed in front of his chest. He never let the amulet out of his sight for even a moment. If Jarok didn't need its magic, he wouldn't even be allowed to touch it.

Jarok left the others to complete the spell and went to William. "It needs to be done. You've spent all your gold, and these people will not work on a promise like I have."

"Soon," William said. "Soon there will be enough monsters roaming the forest that none will dare try to escape. Soon I will have enough sorcerers that Maury will not dare challenge me. Soon—"

"No, William. Not soon. The king has already discovered a way to kill the creatures. We cannot make them as fast as he can kill them. It has to be now. We will take the castle tonight."

William's eyes darkened, but only for a moment. He let out a deep breath. "You have served me well, Jarok. Tomorrow, when I am king, I will name you my head sorcerer."

"Among other things."

William chuckled. "Don't worry. You'll be properly recompensed."

Jarok nodded.

He rejoined the other sorcerers. "Well done." At least two of the three had far more experience than he did, and at first they'd resented his leadership, but William made it clear that Jarok was the head, and the only one he trusted. William's endorsement, coupled with Jarok's gift for transmogrification and his exclusive access to the amulet, made the others willing to fall in line.

"When you're finished, gather your satchels. Every magical artifact and potion you have will be necessary. We attack the castle at midnight."

His eyes fell on the creature they'd conjured. This one appeared to be part cougar with a scorpion's tail and eagle's wings. It was still disoriented from the spell, shaking its furry head back and forth and blinking. It would be several hours before it fully woke, its power and instincts matching its new shape.

The sorcerers dragged it outside to release it into the forest.

The old but spacious cottage Jarok had appropriated for his workshop sat just inside the tree line. The quarters were cramped and uncomfortable with all the sorcerers William had gathered, but no one dared leave the safety of its walls. The creatures wouldn't discriminate between their creators and any other prey. Only William was safe. When they left tonight, it would be under William's protection.

Just before dusk, all seven of them gathered in the main room. William placed himself in the center of the group, the sorcerers huddled around him, as they all shuffled through the door.

Violet eyes lined the path, the forest echoed with snarls as the troupe made its way the short distance to the meadow beyond the trees. From there, they marched on the castle.

Maury's army lined the walls, raining arrows down upon them. They'd prepared for this. Each sorcerer had a gift, and each had a job. Some created a barrier to ward off the arrows, while others worked a spell to open the gate, and more used their staffs to fend off the soldiers who tried to push them back.

It could hardly even be called a battle. A mere human army was no match for Jarok's sorcerers. Once inside, they followed William as he made his way down the long corridor.

A woman peered out from behind a pillar. Jarok glanced at her, wary of danger.

She was just a maid, he saw at once, and she looked terrified. She was no danger. She darted in the opposite direction, a bundle held tightly in her arms.

Something about her made him feel uneasy, as though letting her escape with whatever she'd stolen would change his future, but he pushed the feeling aside. It was just nerves. No need to punish a frightened little girl for taking advantage of the chaos to steal some small comfort for her family.

William had already turned a corner. He shook off the uneasiness and hurried after the rest of the sorcerers.

Another group of soldiers guarded the door to a room at the end of a long hall. A man stood there, protecting the door with his life. Jarok knew instantly he was the king. His features resembled William's, but his chin was firmer, his eyes more authoritative, and his mouth was set in a hard line, not the sardonic twist William usually wore.

"Hello, brother," William said.

"William, please. Let us go. We'll leave peacefully."

William pushed past him and shoved open the door. An old woman stood inside, holding a newborn baby in her arms.

William sauntered toward them. "Congratulations, Maury. You have a son."

"Your nephew," the king said, his tone pleading.

William ignored him. He reached out to touch the baby. The old woman stared, frozen, as William took the child from her. "The firstborn of the king. The heir to the throne."

The queen began sobbing and Maury fell to his knees, begging. "William, please, not my son."

"As I see it, since you are no longer king, you have no need of an heir."

"Yes. Take the crown. We'll leave and you'll never hear from us again. You will be king. You *are* king."

William chuckled. "If only it were that simple. You've already given me the power." He fingered the amethyst that hung from a heavy gold chain around his neck. "However, we both know it's not enough. As long as you are alive, as long as your heir is alive, the crown can never be wholly mine."

"William—brother! Please!"

William pulled a knife from his cloak and plunged it into the child, then into the king.

Jarok felt sick inside, watching William slaughter his brother and nephew. He buried the feeling. He'd chosen his allegiance.

The queen's screams cut off as she fainted.

William finished by sending her to be with her husband and son. He wiped the knife clean on the queen's blanket and looked at the old woman. "You have cared for me since I was a child, and I take no pleasure in killing the infirm. With your pledge of fealty, I will spare your life."

The woman knelt. "I have always served the crown, no matter whose head it rested on."

William nodded and turned away. He pulled the crown from Maury's head and placed it on his own.

Jarok felt the same uneasiness, the same feeling of premonition he'd felt when he saw the maid.

William turned. "It is done." He led the way to the throne room where he took his place upon the throne. The other sorcerers bowed and left the room. Only Jarok remained. He stood by the king's right hand, his proper place as head sorcerer and chief advisor. "Majesty, I have one concern. The old woman, the one who was with the queen—I don't trust her."

"Ada? She's just a midwife. She's harmless."

"She uses magic. I could feel it."

"Yes, but only the smallest bit. She sees glimmers of the future and can make a few simple potions. Don't worry about her."

"She's hiding something."

"Perhaps. But whatever it is, it doesn't concern me. She has no power, not compared to you. She was an ancient old crone when she delivered me. I expect she'll not live long, but she will be loyal to me for as long as she's here."

Jarok decided not to press the point further, but he would watch her very carefully. If she had a secret, he would find it.

Revolution

The queen's screams filled the room with their violence, and were answered by shouts from the army that protected the castle.

Ada bathed the queen's head in cool water. "It's almost time, now. Just a little longer."

The queen screeched again as another contraction gripped her.

Ada felt the queen's stomach. "Very good, Your Majesty. Your son will be here soon."

She nodded toward the young serving girl, ordered to help but completely at a loss for what to do, who stood in the corner wringing her hands. "Come hold her hand. Keep her cool. I'll be right back."

She shuffled down the corridor and out to the front hall. The king's personal guards stood by the door, the last line of defense. At their center, she found King Maury. "Your Majesty, what is happening?"

Maury looked at her, his eyes vacant. "We are being attacked. A band of sorcerers is very quickly demolishing our army. Any minute they'll breach the gate. How is my wife?"

"I have rarely seen a woman work so hard to bring a life into the world. But I believe she and the babe will make it through this and be healthy."

"Good. Stay by her side. Be ready. If the sorcerers break through, you will hide my wife and the baby and keep them safe."

Ada bowed. "I will do what I can."

She made her way back to the queen's chambers. The queen screamed in agony as Ada reentered the room. Ada smiled. "It is time. Your son is coming. Keep pushing now."

Several excruciating minutes later, the infant was born. Ada lifted the child, then stopped.

41

What devilry was this?

Had the sorcerers somehow bewitched the queen? Ada had seen clearly in a vision that the queen would bear a son, but the child in her arms was a beautiful baby girl.

She snapped her jaw shut. No sense in letting the queen see her anxiety.

She swaddled the child and laid her on the queen's chest. "Congratulations, Your Majesty. You have a daughter."

The look of rapture on the queen's face dispelled any fears Ada had about her reaction to the child's gender.

Suddenly the queen groaned, clutching her stomach.

"Don't fret," Ada soothed. "It's just the afterbirth."

Ada took the baby and handed her to the maidservant, then turned back toward the queen. "Another few minutes, and then it will be over."

A crash from somewhere down the hall made her jump.

"Be ready!" King Maury's voice. "They've breached the castle. Protect the queen at all costs!"

There was no time to think, only to act. Ada swept all the gold in the room and the queen's jewels into a blanket and tied it at the top, then thrust it at the serving girl. "Take the baby. Use the back stairs and get out of the palace, quickly. You must care for her until I come get her. Keep her safe, no matter what."

The girl stood, frozen, clutching the baby and the bundle of jewels to her chest.

Ada slapped her.

She stumbled back, shock on her face.

Ada didn't have time to be gentle. "Go now. Use the gold to buy whatever you need. Just keep the baby safe."

The maid turned and fled through the servant's entrance, the echo of her footsteps drowned out by another of the queen's screams.

Ada turned to her patient.

What she saw made her breath stop.

It couldn't be! She would have seen it!

She hurried to the queen's side. "There, there, Majesty. Push once more."

The door slammed open and King Maury backed in, his hands stretched out in front of him as if to slow the wave of sorcerers that pushed through.

A wave led by King Maury's own brother.

William strode over to the bed just as the queen delivered a second baby into Ada's waiting arms.

Ada held the baby close and eyed William.

William sauntered toward them. "Congratulations, Maury. You have a son."

"Your nephew," Maury said, his tone pleading.

William ignored him. He reached out to touch the baby, his hand brushing Ada's as he did so.

A vision tore through Ada's mind, searing, violent. She wanted to weep, but the horrors were too vivid. William, rampaging for years and years, destroying everyone who stood against him, with no one to stop the spread of his evil.

Ada could only stare, frozen, as William took the child from her.

"The firstborn of the king. The heir to the throne."

The queen began sobbing, and Maury fell to his knees, begging. "William, please, not my son."

Ada whispered an enchantment over the baby, to protect him from magic, but her head still throbbed from her vision, and the spell was weak.

"As I see it, since you are no longer king, you have no need of an heir."

William's eyes burned with hate. The amulet around his neck

sparked with the same evil glow.

The amulet.

Just as she was about to tell Maury to take it, the knowledge came to her that he couldn't. Nor could she. The power of the amulet was bonded to William through a powerful spell.

That day, weeks ago, in the woods. Maury had met with William.

Ada closed her eyes as another wave of blindingly painful visions overwhelmed her. The amulet pulled her. She could no more deny it than she could deny her soul. She knew what William was about to do, yet she could not stop it.

"William—brother! Please!"

William stepped toward Ada. She held the baby to her chest, but her legs stood rooted to the spot, compelled by William's will, amplified through the amulet, and shooting through her. William pulled a knife from his cloak and plunged it into the child.

Any hope Ada had of thwarting the visions of William's tyrannical rule poured out like the blood that ran from the infant.

William turned toward Maury who stood frozen and plunged the knife into his chest.

The queen's screams cut off as she fainted. William was no more gentle with her than he had been with the infant. He wiped the knife clean on the queen's blanket and looked at Ada. "You have cared for me since I was a child, and I take no pleasure in killing the infirm. With your pledge of fealty, I will spare your life."

Ada knelt on sore, creaking knees. She could not resist, no matter how much she wanted to. "I have always served the crown, no matter whose head it rested on."

William nodded and turned away. He knelt next to Maury's body. No trace of compassion or regret marred his features as he yanked the crown from Maury's head and placed it on his own.

"I swear to you my fealty, my king." Ada spoke the words, and she had no choice but to follow them. She only prayed that one day this evil could be righted, that Maury's true firstborn would one day defeat the evil she saw in her vision. She prayed the child would be safe with Margaret.

Uprising

Twenty Years after William Took the Throne

Rina pulled the misshapen, withered carrot from dry earth and put it in the basket. She glanced around the garden at the plants that fought to grow, and beyond, to the fields that stretched on, with sparse yellow grass and dry dusty earth, to the forest. The trees there were still bright and green, seemingly unaffected by the drought that plagued the land and seemed to worsen every year.

She looked at her mother. "I remember when I was a child, these used to be plump and straight. Is my imagination so rosy I don't even remember vegetables accurately?"

Margaret chuckled. "No, it's not your imagination. Fruit and vegetables were more abundant then."

"What happened?"

"No one really knows. The land has been in decline for the last twenty years, or so. Some think it's because of all the magic."

Rina stood and brushed the dirt from her dress. "What does magic have to do with vegetables getting smaller and the land becoming less productive?"

"I can't claim to understand it all myself, but sometimes the sorcerers who come to drink at the tavern speak of it. The power of magic comes from nature. Sorcerers draw from the elements, harnessing that power to perform their spells."

Rina looked toward the castle. It looked small from so far away, but her mother had taken her there once when she was little. It was as big as the entire South Village, encompassed all around with a looming stone wall.

The Seven lived there, doing the king's bidding. Rina had never met one. They rarely left the confines of the castle except on business

46

for the king, so it surprised her to hear her mother speak of them so casually.

Were they using magic now? Was her basket of carrots suffering because of some silly spell? "Using magic destroys everything around? Why would the king allow such a thing?"

Margaret brushed a lock of hair from her forehead, leaving a streak of dirt in the beads of sweat that dotted her forehead. "It's not supposed to be like that. Normally, there is so much energy, a little magic actually helps to maintain balance. However, so many sorcerers all in one place, performing so many spells, has depleted the elements."

"Why doesn't the king put a stop to it, then?"

"Perhaps he doesn't realize what is happening." Margaret glanced over her shoulder, as though to check to make sure no one was nearby. "Or, more likely, he fears to rule without the aid of magic. The only reason he holds the throne is because he used magic to obtain it. But you must never repeat that. The king considers any such talk to be treason."

Margaret stood and brushed the dirt from her skirt. "I need to get cleaned up before work."

Rina stood and followed her to the cottage. "Why do you still work at the tavern? Tommin is a cruel taskmaster. We could use—"

Margaret whirled around and clapped a hand over Rina's mouth. "Stop. Don't speak of it. Don't even think of it. That is for you, when you get older. I will not spend a speck of it."

Margaret hurried inside. "The tavern isn't so bad. Tommin has let me continue on, even though I'm not as young as I once was. I've been able to provide comfortably for you, and that's all I ever wanted."

Rina began to prepare the evening meal. She scrubbed the carrots and other wilted vegetables and put them in the pot with a little bit of salted pork.

The king's sorcerers were destroying the land. The people were beginning to suffer. The king either didn't notice or didn't care.

Rina knew little of other lands. Margaret had taught her to read, but the availability of books was scarce. She had no idea how it was done in other kingdoms, but something felt…wrong.

It wasn't just that her mother warned her against speaking treason. Everyone in all the Villages knew not to speak out against the King or the Seven. It went deeper, a tugging at her heart, telling her that the way the king ruled wasn't what it should be.

The king's duty was to his kingdom, his people. But King William cared only for himself, his own power. Therefore, a new king needed to be installed, one who would protect and care for the people, not destroy them to protect himself.

She didn't have any idea who the new king should be, only that the current one had to be overthrown. It seemed so simple.

Rina and her mother ate in silence, and after the meal, when Margaret left for her job at the tavern, Rina went to see an old friend.

She sat on the top rung of the fence swinging her legs while Troy paced in front of her.

"What you're suggesting is treason. You could be hanged for this. I could be hanged just for listening."

"You know I'm right, Troy. We need a new king. Furthermore, I'm sure I can't be the only one who thinks so."

"You can't just replace him. He's the *king*."

"Why? What makes him so special?"

Troy rolled his eyes. "You already know the answer to that. The land is inextricably linked to the Legerdemain bloodline."

"But why? Who says it has to be that way?"

"Without a royal heir to rule, the land would not survive."

"So says the king. But maybe he's just saying that to keep from being killed before he can father an heir."

"Rina, stop. As a member of the king's royal guard, I'm sworn to protect both king and kingdom."

"What if protecting one is at the cost of destroying the other?" Rina jumped from the fence and took Troy's hand. "The land is already on the brink of desolation. Perhaps the land will die without him, but it is just as likely to die *because* of him. If he will not do his duty to save this land and these people, someone else must at least try."

"Who do you have in mind?"

Rina shrugged. "I don't know yet. But I know I can't be the only one who thinks this way. Even you agree with me, and you're in the King's Guard."

Troy shrugged. "It's the highest paying job a guy can get without knowing magic."

"So will you help me?"

Troy squeezed her hand. "You know I'd do anything for you."

***

Three nights later, in a cottage at the edge of the village, Rina stood before a small group of men and women she and Troy had recruited. She explained her reasoning, how the king had failed the land and the time for change was at hand. "We need to kill the king. With him dead and no one to pay their wages, the sorcerers will disband."

"It's not that easy," one man said. "The king is surrounded by sorcerers at all times. They use magic to test his food and create magical barriers against attack. Moreover, even if we succeed in killing the king, what is to keep the sorcerers from taking control?"

"I agree," another man said. "You are young and idealistic, but do you really think this hasn't been thought of before? It won't work. You need a plan to get rid of the sorcerers and to keep more from coming."

Mutters of agreement rose up around the room. "There's no way to get rid of the sorcerers," someone said.

"Even sorcerers won't work for free. Once the king is dead, the

49

sorcerers will leave."

"And if they don't?" someone else asked.

"Then we'll kill them, too."

The room erupted in laughter.

Rina crossed her arms in front of her chest. "Sorcerers are just people. They have weaknesses, just like everyone else."

No one was listening.

Rina bit her lip. She knew what had to be done, but she couldn't do it alone and she was losing this crowd.

Troy stepped forward. "The time has come. We can no longer sit back and watch our land be destroyed. Rina isn't suggesting it will be easy, but it is necessary. We need to formulate a plan together. That's why we called you all here. Who is willing to rise up with us?"

The room was silent for a long time.

Rina looked nervously from Troy to the group before her.

Someone at the back moved, a gentle shuffling as he made his way forward. He was in his middle years, limping, leaning heavily on a cane, but his eyes were sharp and his voice clear when he spoke. "My name is Graydon, my lady."

Rina blushed. She'd never been called "my lady" before.

Graydon stood in front of her. "I was there the day the king took the throne. I failed in my duty to protect the former king. I watched as William murdered his brother, his sister-in-law, and his infant nephew. It is long past time someone had the courage to stand up against him."

"Thank you, Graydon."

"It will not be easy. You need a leader, someone who is able to train and lead troops, someone the people will follow into battle and support as the new king. Until you have those things, all your plans will fall flat. These people cannot risk their families for a half-baked idea."

Rina nodded. "Will you lead us?"

Graydon shook his head. "I am too old. I will help and I will consult, but I am not a leader."

Rina looked at Troy. He was the next most ideal candidate, but the panic in his eyes gave her pause. He would follow her to the ends of the earth, but she could not ask him to lead a cause he didn't believe in.

She looked at the faces before her, lingering a moment on each individual, searching for any sign of commitment. "Who will agree to lead us? To make the hard decisions, no matter the cost?"

No one moved.

Tears stung Rina's eyes, but she blinked them back. She would not show weakness. She brought these people here, and she would see it through.

Perhaps Graydon would reconsider. She turned to him, ready to plead if necessary. "Please, Graydon. You are the only one with the ability and experience to be our leader."

Graydon smiled. "No, my lady. You are." He lowered himself slowly to his knees before Rina and bowed his head. "Whatever plan you devise, I will follow. Whatever orders you give, I will carry out. I swear to you my allegiance, Lady Rina. Lead me to battle. Save this land."

Leader

"I can't lead these people, Troy. I don't have the first idea of what I'm doing."

Troy stood behind Rina in the barn, showing her how to stand, how to hold a sword. "Then quit."

"I can't quit."

"Why not? Just tell the people you realized you were wrong, and it's better to obey the king."

She whirled to face him. "I'm *not* wrong. The king is wrong."

Troy grinned.

"You knew I'd say that."

He nodded. "Do you think it's coincidence that you spoke up when you did? The people have been suffering under King William for twenty years. They've been waiting for someone to follow, even if they didn't know it." He turned her back around and repositioned the sword.

Rina stepped in tandem with Troy, allowing him to lead her steps as she danced through the sequence. Her arms ached from holding the heavy, two-handed sword, but Troy wouldn't let her give up. "I'm just the daughter of a tavern wench. I have no right to tell them what to do."

"A leader is only a leader if people follow. All the qualifications in the world won't make a leader out of someone no one trusts. But they trust you."

"That's a lot of responsibility. I'm not sure I'm ready for it."

"You started this revolution, Rina. You don't have the option to not be ready."

Rina lowered her arms and turned to face him. "What if I fail?"

"Then people will die, and the king will build up his defenses, which will make it that much harder for the next person who tries."

She frowned at him. "Thanks for making it easy on me."

Troy took the sword from her and set it against a post. He took her hands in his and looked into her eyes. "It's not going to be easy. People will die. But it needs to be done. The kingdom is at a turning point, one way or the other. Whether you meant to or not, you put yourself at the center, and now it's your responsibility to see it through."

Rina blinked. "I guess I never thought it would go this far. Or at least, that I'd be responsible for everyone. I thought I'd help. I thought I'd rally the people and share ideas. I didn't want to be the one everyone was counting on."

"But you are. So you have to ask yourself, are you prepared to do what needs to be done? Are you willing to step up to the role fate has handed you? Or are you going to let everyone down?"

Rina laid her head on Troy's chest. "I don't know if I'm ready. But I'm willing to do what it takes to become ready. I'm won't let my people down."

Troy lifted her face with his fingertips and softly kissed her forehead. "And that is why they need you."

She stepped back. "Can we work with knives again? I feel much more comfortable with something small."

Troy nodded and handed her a set of knives. He positioned her hand and pointed at a post a few yards away. "Aim for that knot."

An hour later, Rina's arms felt like they were likely to fall off, but she consistently hit at least close to where she aimed. "I need to rest," she said finally.

"I have to go back to the castle tonight. I won't be back for a week," Troy told her. "Keep practicing, and we'll spar when I return."

"Thank you, Troy." Rina slipped her hand into his. "I couldn't do this without you. Let me treat you to dinner at the tavern."

Troy agreed, but Rina knew it was only because her mother would feed them both for free.

They sat at the table in the corner and talked in low tones.

Margaret served them each a bowl of watery stew and a thin slice of bread, then left them to themselves.

"I'll borrow books from the castle library. No one will miss them, but you'll need to know the history of Legerdemain as well as some of the surrounding countries if you're going to be a good leader," Troy said.

Rina rubbed her head. "This is much more complicated than I thought it would be."

"Whatever it takes, remember?"

Rina opened her mouth to respond, but stopped when the door to the tavern burst open.

A man came in, herding a very pregnant woman.

He dropped a few coins on the counter and pushed them toward Tommin, the tavern keeper. "Whatever food that will buy. Bread and grain, if possible, and put it in sacks, please."

Tommin shuffled toward the kitchen.

"Please hurry," the man said.

The woman glanced out the window and tugged at the man's arm. "He's coming."

The man looked frantically around the room. "The king's guard...I just took a little food from the kitchen. The baby will come soon, and she needed her strength. Someone, please..." his voice trailed off as people in the tavern averted their eyes.

Rina looked at Troy.

"They're your people, now. Whatever it takes."

Rina stood and beckoned toward the man and woman. "This way."

They hurried after her. Rina led them down the hallway to the back storeroom.

She and Troy had played back there countless times when they were little and Margaret was working.

In the back, behind the barrels of ale, was a small hole in the wall. Tommin had never bothered to have it properly repaired, only covered it with a flap of cow hide. Rina had discovered it once and used it to trick Troy for months before he figured it out.

She moved a crate of potatoes and lifted the flap. "It will be tight, but you should be able to fit."

The man knelt and poked his head through, turning back and forth, looking for any sign of the guard, then slithered through.

Rina helped the woman lower herself down and roll to her side to squeeze through without putting pressure on the baby. Her husband pulled from the other side and in a moment she was free.

Rina looked through the hole. "There's a tree in the South Pasture, the biggest one in sight for miles. Meet me at the last cottage in the village before you reach the tree."

The man nodded his agreement and bustled the woman away.

Rina stood and brushed the dust from her dress and smoothed her hair. She rolled an empty cask in front of the hole and put the potatoes on top of it.

She glanced around again, grabbed a jug of cider, then hurried to the main room. "I found it. The last one. It's really time to restock, Tommin, or people will start going to the West Village to drink."

She feigned looking around the room at the faces that cowered before the guardsman. "What's going on?'

The guardsman stepped toward her. "Two fugitives, on the run from the king's justice. Have you seen them?"

Rina lifted the jug. "The only thing I've seen is this cider. Let me buy you a glass, before it's all gone."

The guardsman eyed her. "You're sure they're not back there?"

"The only thing back there is old potatoes." She turned, set the jug on the counter, and pushed it toward her mother. "One for me and one for the king's guard, to moisten his lips before he continues his search."

The guard strode down the hallway and peered in the storage room.

Rina's heart thudded against her chest as she held her cup of cider to her lips.

The guard returned a moment later and took the mug she offered him. "You'll let me know if you see them."

"Of course." She took a sip, her eyes never leaving the guard as he chugged down his drink, slammed his mug on the counter, and sauntered out.

A collective sigh of relief rose up around the room when the door slammed shut behind him.

"What are you doing?" Tommin hissed.

Rina just stared at him. "The food the man paid for. Do you have it?"

Tommin thrust a satchel at her.

Rina looked around the room. "By morning those two will be gone, as if they were never here. None of you saw them. Understood?"

Several people nodded, but most sat in silence.

"You're going to get us all killed," Tommin said.

Rina studied his face. Why hadn't he betrayed her?

Margaret put a hand on Tommin's shoulder. "If anyone could have, they would've done the same for Roselle."

Tommin's mouth tightened in a hard line. He gave a curt nod. "Get 'em out of here and don't come back."

Rina grabbed the satchel and hurried home.

The man and his wife huddled in the back behind a wilted bush. She led them inside. "You can stay here until I can find a way to get you out of the kingdom."

The front door crashed open.

The king's guardsman stood there, grinning. "I knew there was something funny about you."

"Get back," Rina yelled, pushing the pregnant woman behind her. She backed further into the main room.

The guard stalked toward her. "Now I get to turn over three traitors instead of two. This'll be a pretty bounty."

Rina edged away from the man and his wife, backing into the wall on the opposite side of the room.

She held the guardsman's gaze as she reached out slowly with one had to where the dishes were stacked on the shelf by her side.

Her hand tightened around the hilt of her mother's cooking knife.

In one swift motion, she positioned it the way Troy had taught her and hurled it at the guardsman.

He stumbled forward, clutching the knife in his chest, and collapsed to the floor.

She walked slowly toward him and nudged him with her foot. He didn't move. When she rolled him over, vacant eyes stared up at her.

She looked up at the man. "There's a bed in the room to the left. Your wife can lie down, and then you can help me move his body. We'll leave it in the forest for the monsters."

The man walked his wife into the bedroom. Rina pulled the knife from the guard's chest, wiped it clean on his coat, and stuck it into her sash. She'd never be without it again.

Assassin

The body hung from a pike in the center of the town square, high enough that it could be seen from beyond the village. The pike was guarded by a sorcerer, so none could cut it down. It hung there, flesh torn, dangling in unnatural positions from countless broken bones.

Rina gagged, depositing what little she'd had to eat in the brown grass in the field outside the village.

Margaret woke her in the middle of the night to inform her that Graydon, the first man to follow Rina, to swear his allegiance to her, had been captured.

"Someone heard him talking in the tavern," Margaret said. "Trying to convince people to join him."

Before Rina could even plan a rescue, the king's sorcerers had done this to him.

Composing herself, Rina made her way to the center of town. She looked around to see if anyone was watching, but the square was empty. Shutters were closed and the streets were deserted. No one wanted to risk looking sympathetic.

She slowly approached the sorcerer who stood guard. "How long must you leave him up there? There are children in this town. They shouldn't see things like that."

"He is there to serve as a warning."

"A warning against what?"

"Plotting against the king."

"Who would plot against the king?"

"Rest assured, young lady, we will find out."

Rina jerked her head toward the corpse. "He didn't tell you?"

"Not a word."

"Even after all that..." Her words caught in her throat as she imagined Graydon enduring endless agony as his bones were systematically broken, his flesh torn in an attempt to get him to talk.

The sorcerer shook his head. "He didn't say a word." He gave a low, sinister chuckle. "We enjoyed trying, though. And the same will happen to anyone else who plots treason against the king."

Almost before she realized what she was doing, Rina pulled her knife from her belt and thrust it into the sorcerer's heart.

No one had ever challenged a sorcerer. The people were too afraid of the magic they wielded. No sorcerer had ever had reason to fear his own safety. The look of surprise in the sorcerer's eyes as he clutched his chest told Rina just how confident he'd been in his own powers.

Rina pulled out the knife and slashed it across his throat. He crumbled to the ground, his life ebbing from him.

His cloak fell open, revealing a pouch tucked into an inside pocket. Rina pulled it out, expecting gold. Instead, she found a number of strange objects. A small bag of grayish green powder, other bags containing various herbs and dried leaves, a tooth she could only assume once belonged to a wild animal, a scroll covered in strange writing, a vial of some type of potion, and several other items she couldn't begin to define.

She knew nothing of magic, but these things might be useful at some point. She tucked the pouch into her belt and stood up. She had to get Graydon's body down.

She borrowed an axe from the woodpile behind the tavern and began to hack at the pole. Before long she'd carved a notch, and the weight of the body made the pole bend. She pulled it lower, slowly lowering the body to the ground. She stood over him and let the tears fall. He was the first casualty in the war she'd started.

She took the sorcerer's cloak and wrapped Graydon's body in it. She couldn't carry it by herself, though, and she didn't want to risk anyone else's life by asking for help.

Her mother had a cart. If she could get him on that…

"Rina, what did you do?"

Rina whirled around.

Troy stood behind her, staring at the dead sorcerer.

"I killed him."

"There's no going back from this."

"I know. But I know the king's weakness now. Will you help me bury Graydon?"

Troy lifted Graydon's body over one shoulder and took the sorcerer by one hand. "Get his other hand and help me pull."

Together they transported the two bodies to Margaret's cart. Troy hoisted the bodies onto it and wheeled it down the road. They dumped the guard just inside the edge of the forest, as Rina had done with the last guard, then wheeled Graydon to the field of graves beyond the village.

Rina and Troy took turns with the one shovel. Blisters covered Rina's hands and sweat and dirt blinded her. At last, the hole was deep enough to lay Graydon in it.

Rina pulled a small gem from the pouch of magical artifacts she'd retrieved from the sorcerer and laid it on Graydon's chest. "May you receive rewards in the next life for your service in this one," she said softly.

Scoop by scoop, Troy filled the hole back in.

"Let me help," Rina said.

Troy just smiled. "Save your strength. You'll need it."

When at last the hole was filled, Troy slipped an arm around Rina's waist and pulled her close. Tired and sore as she was, she could only imagine how exhausted Troy must be. Together, they limped back toward Rina's cottage.

Once inside, she pointed to a chair. "Sit." She soaked a soft cloth in water and began washing Troy's blistered hands.

Troy leaned against the chair's back and closed his eyes. "What is your plan?"

"I can't tell you."

Troy sat up. "Rina, you can't do this alone."

"I have to. I won't let what happened to Graydon happen to anyone else." She looked into his eyes and lightly stroked his face with her fingertips. "Especially you."

"Rina—"

"No. I have to do this. Like you said, there's no going back now. But I won't drag the rest of Legerdemain with me if I can help it."

***

Rina sat at a table at the back of the tavern, alone, and watched the patrons. Townspeople sat around the edge of the room, looking furtively toward the center tables where a group of sorcerers chatted and laughed together. They had not yet discovered the truth about their fallen comrade. Rina had let slip a rumor about a pretty girl and too much wine, and the sorcerer on guard letting Graydon's body disappear.

No one questioned it. Like the one she'd killed this morning, these sorcerers believed themselves invulnerable. A few thought whoever took Graydon's body should be punished, but most argued the lesson had been learned and feared no further trouble from a half-hearted attempt at revolution.

Late in the evening, one of the sorcerers got up from the table and wobbled on unsteady feet toward the door.

Rina waited a moment, then threw her cloak over her shoulders, pulled the hood up so it covered her face, and followed.

The sorcerer tramped to the better part of the village and into a spacious house. The house of someone well-to-do. A merchant? His lover, perhaps? Or had he decided he'd had enough of living under the king's constant watch and appropriated this house for himself?

The sight of this murderous sorcerer living in a house twice the size and ten times as ornate as any of the hard-working villagers filled Rina with cold hate. She stood outside the door until the lights had been extinguished and all was quiet within.

The sorcerer hadn't even bothered to bar the door, and Rina snuck in silently.

She entered into an enormous foyer, nearly as large as her entire cottage, and tiptoed past an ornate fireplace. No fire burned in it—the weather was too hot for that—but when it was lit, it would light up the whole room, illuminating finely crafted furniture and gilt decorations.

She padded through the house until she found the hallway that led to several bedrooms. The first two were empty, but at the end of the hall she found the sorcerer sleeping, snoring loudly. She crept to the side of the bed and looked at him. Without another thought, she plunged her knife into the sorcerer's heart.

The king's weakness was in what he thought was his greatest strength: his sorcerers. Together, they were a mighty force to protect the king. Apart, they could be killed as easily as any man. Rina would defeat the king by destroying his army of sorcerers. One by one, she would kill them all.

Visions

"Dead? What do you mean, dead?" The king's voice, cold and raspy, sent a chill through Ada, filling her with a terror more complete than if he'd screamed.

"Murdered. Stabbed through the heart in his bed. I saw it. A runner will be here within the hour to inform you."

"How is it possible that an assassin could sneak up on a sorcerer and murder him in his bed?"

"I cannot say, Majesty."

"You have one purpose, and that is to see. If you do not fulfill that, then why should I let you live?"

"I will try again, Majesty."

Ada bowed and shuffled from the room. Down the corridor, to the servants chambers, then below, through a dimly lit hallway to her chamber.

She prepared the herbs, mixed them in the bowl, and called forth the vision she'd seen earlier.

A figure in a black cloak crept into the darkened room. The sorcerer's home was remarkably ordinary. The furnishings were costly, but uninteresting. But for the closet filled with witchery, it could have been the cottage of any well-to-do merchant. The sorcerer was a man in his middle years, dark-haired, snoring through a hooked nose.

The cloaked figure approached the bed and raised a knife. The sorcerer snorted and shifted in his sleep. The assassin paused, knife raised, until the sorcerer settled back into rest, then plunged the knife into his chest.

As the figure turned, Ada caught a glimpse of a face, pale and smooth, obscured by shadow. A young boy? Or a woman?

The vision started to fade. This was where she'd lost it before.

She focused her energy and held on to the image. The assassin went to the closet and pawed through its contents, finally selecting a bottle and hiding it in a satchel. The hood of the cloak fell away, revealing the face.

A woman, barely beyond girlhood.

There was something familiar about her. Ada was certain she'd seen the girl before, but where or when, she couldn't place.

The vision faded then, and Ada was back in her chamber. "Who are you, Girl?" she asked aloud. "Why did you kill him? A personal vendetta? You were a lover scorned, perhaps? Or were you hired? And if so, by whom?"

Ada mixed more herbs, created another potion, and looked into her bowl again.

The picture that formed was of the future. The same girl, the assassin, rigged some sort of trap on the North Road, just before it reached the forest. A short while later, a carriage came along the road. The horse stumbled, the trap sprung, and a tree fell, crushing the top of the carriage. From inside, a woman screamed. The assassin girl ran toward the carriage. "Are you hurt?" she called out.

"No, I'm just trapped," the woman inside answered.

"I'll see if I can help," the girl said.

"No need. Stand back."

There was a rumble of thunder, then the carriage shook and broke apart. A tall, elegant woman emerged from the rubble, her rich gown torn and dirty, but she was otherwise unhurt. The residue of her spell hung around her like an aura.

The girl assassin rushed forward. "Is there anything I can do?"

The sorceress smiled at the look of awe on the girl's face. "Thank you, child, but I'm quite all right."

"At least let me take care of your horse. He looks frightened out of his wits. Come, you can stay at my home to be refreshed until a replacement carriage can be summoned."

The sorceress nodded. "Thank you."

The girl unharnessed the horse and led it toward the sorceress. "Will you ride or walk?"

"I'll ride."

"Let me help you up." The girl stood behind the sorceress, making as though to boost her onto the horse's back. Then, hands moving so fast Ada scarcely saw what was happening, she pulled a knife from her belt and shoved it in the sorceress's back. Straight through the heart.

The sorceress fell back, gurgling, almost on top of the girl. The girl stepped out of the way and let her fall to the ground. She then searched the woman's body until she found a pouch hanging from the woman's belt. Using her knife, the girl cut the pouch loose and stuffed it in her satchel. She took the horse and left the sorceress's body lying by the side of the road.

Ada let the vision fade.

After the first two sorcerers had disappeared, the king had sent summons all over the world for men and women who could practice magic. They had come, little by little, but as fast as they came, this girl killed them.

Intentionally.

But why?

Ada concocted one final potion, attempting to see into the motives of the assassin.

She looked into the bowl and was confronted with such a barrage of images she was thrown backward.

A purple gem, dripping with blood.

A monster that haunted the forest running in fear of something even worse.

Herself, and everyone in the palace, in the city, the villages—everyone in the whole country writhing in agony, burning from fire falling from the sky.

When she woke, Ada was lying on her back on the stone floor. The candle had burned almost to a nub and her head throbbed. Tears streamed down her face as the truth of the future overwhelmed her.

If the girl assassin got her hands on the amulet, the kingdom and everyone in it would be destroyed.

The Forest

"Are you mad? You can't go into the forest!"

Rina finished folding supplies into her blanket and tied it into a knapsack. She embraced Margaret. "I have to. The king will keep hunting me, and more of the people I love will die trying to protect me."

"But the creatures—they'll tear you apart."

"Better me than someone else."

"Rina, please. Don't go."

Rina took the hand of the woman who'd raised her. "The king will not stop until I'm dead. Or, worse, until he has killed everyone I love. That means you. But even he is afraid to go in the forest. Somehow, I'll find a way to survive there."

"But what about the people who depend on you? You are the only one fighting against the king. What will we do without you?"

"I'll still lead them. I'll just have a different domain to command from."

Tears formed in the older woman's eyes. "Be careful."

Rina embraced her one last time. "I will. I'll find a way to let you know when I'm safe."

***

Rina looked up at the trees that towered before her.

Since before her birth, no one who had ventured into those woods had returned. The monsters that resided therein devoured any who tried to escape. The only road through the forest to the world beyond was guarded by the king's sorcerers. The king made certain that his people could never leave.

For a moment, her courage failed, but she thought of Margaret. She couldn't bear the thought of the king doing to Margaret what he'd done to the last person caught helping Rina form a resistance. Images of the man's remains still haunted Rina's nightmares.

Worse than what they'd done to Graydon. The man's body had been unrecognizable. Pieces of it had been delivered to the Four Villages along with threats that the same would happen to anyone else caught helping the assassin who killed the king's sorcerers.

The only way to keep her loved ones safe was to take her chances in the forest.

"Rina!"

Rina turned toward the voice that called out to her. "Troy, what are you doing here?"

"Margaret came to me as soon as you left. She told me what you're doing."

"My mind is made up. Don't try to stop me."

"I'm not. I'm coming with you."

"Troy, no. It's too dangerous."

"Which is why you shouldn't be alone."

Rina considered arguing with him, making him go back. But in truth, she wanted his company. The dark shadows of the trees seemed somehow less threatening with him by her side.

"Let's go. We need to get as far into the interior as possible and find a place to camp."

They trekked for a long while, pushing their way through dense underbrush, deeper into the heart of the forest. It was nearing evening when they finally came to a stream.

Rina glanced up and down the bank until she spotted a flat area between two towering pines.

"There," she pointed. "Come on."

Troy looked around at the clearing, his gaze traveling to the dense undergrowth beyond. "Why haven't they attacked?"

Rina followed his gaze. It did seem strange, that after all the stories of the beasts in the woods devouring anyone who entered, not one had yet accosted them. "I don't know. I'm just grateful."

"It doesn't make sense. They must know we're here."

"Maybe they're not hungry. Come on, we need to build a shelter."

"Shelter won't do us any good if the creatures attack us in our sleep. You may be right, though. I've heard reports of people trying to flee the villages since the king brought in the new sorcerers. If they went through the forest, it's possible the creatures really are sated."

Despite his words, Troy helped gather large branches and drag them to the center of the clearing.

Using a thick oak at the edge of the clearing as a support, Rina and Troy formed a log cabin of sorts and covered it over with leaves to serve as thatch.

"You won't defeat the king in here," Troy said after awhile.

"I don't plan on staying here forever. I just need a little space to figure out my next step without endangering my followers."

"If you stay away too long, you won't have any followers."

"Maybe that's better."

Troy stopped working and put his arms around her, pulling her close. "You know that's not true."

Rina wrapped her arms around his waist and leaned her head against his chest. "Isn't it? So far I've managed to get two people killed, and I've let the king reinforce his stronghold by bringing in countless new sorcerers."

"He brought in new sorcerers because he's afraid of you. You hold a certain type of power with that fear. And you have the loyalty of the people. He may control their actions, and whether or not they can leave, but you possess their hearts."

Rina took a deep breath. "I couldn't do this without you."

"I know."

Rina could hear the teasing laughter in his voice, and she hugged him tighter.

"Our shelter is about as good as it can be for now, and it's getting dark. We should rest."

They built a fire, and then Rina pulled bread and meat from her pack of provisions and handed some to Troy.

"Now what?" he asked as he ate. "We sit here and wait to be eaten?"

"No. We build a safe area. The creatures don't come out of the forest to attack the farms or the towns. I think they have some sort of magical restraint that forces them to stay within the bounds of the forest. So, we clean out a space in the forest that they can't enter."

"I don't think it works that way. We're still in the forest."

Rina shrugged. "Then we'll figure out how to kill them."

"Right, because *that* hasn't been tried before."

Rina smiled. "I stole magic from every one of the king's magicians that I killed. My hope is that the magic that created them will somehow be able to destroy them."

"Will that work?"

"It's the only chance I—shh! Listen!"

Rina held her breath, ears straining.

"I don't hear anything," Troy whispered.

"That's the problem. No crickets, no night birds—it's too quiet."

She stood and pulled her sword from its scabbard, nodding to Troy to do the same. She opened the pouch she carried on her belt and pulled out a pinch of the iridescent powder inside.

"Be ready," she whispered.

She and Troy stood back-to-back, swords drawn, waiting.

Something rustled the bushes. Rina turned toward the sound.

A pair of violet eyes glowed in the dark, drawing nearer.

A head like the head of a dragon began to take shape, the glow of the fire illuminating its glistening fangs and dancing in its eyes.

Rina waited until it came a little closer, creeping on its huge, taloned feet, then flung the powder from the pouch at it.

The creature screeched, rising up on its hind legs and lunging toward Rina.

She swiped at it with her sword, but though she felt the blade strike, the blow didn't even seem to slow the creature.

Troy, from the other side, thrust his sword toward the creature's heart.

The monster turned and slashed at him with a claw, tearing through clothes and skin. Troy screamed and fell backward. The creature licked the blood on its claws, and then roared. The blood drove it into a frenzy, and it launched itself at Troy, jaws gaping.

"No!" Rina jumped in front of the creature's head. Its jaws snapped down on her arm.

Rina screamed. She gave a half-hearted attempt to swing her sword, despite her wound, but the pain was overwhelming. It didn't matter. Any moment, the monster would finish her.

But the moment never came.

The creature released her arm, hissing and screeching as though in great pain.

Rina pushed herself to a stand and lunged toward the creature with her sword.

Blood from her wounded arm splashed onto the blade as she thrust toward the creature's exposed chest.

This time, the sword sliced cleanly through the beast's skin.

The creature stumbled backward, roaring.

What? How?

She glanced at her torn arm, at the blood that smeared on her blade, and at the monster that writhed on the ground before her.

Why did her blood repel it, when Troy's had drawn it?

It didn't matter, at least not now. Now, she had to finish the beast.

Rina wiped more blood on the tip of the sword and chased after the creature, stabbing it again and again until it finally toppled over.

She collapsed against it, exhausted. Its blood and hers dripped into the ground.

She'd killed it. Instead of becoming the forest's victim, she had figured out how to conquer it. By accident, to be sure, but still, it was an important achievement.

At least if she could kill the monsters, she'd be safe in the forest, and that gave her an advantage over the king and even the sorcerers.

More violet eyes peered at her through the dense foliage. Even though she now knew the trick, she didn't have the energy to fight another one tonight. She stood and waved her bloody sword at the creature that stalked her.

It emitted a low growl, but didn't come near her.

She glanced down at the creature she'd killed. Its hide would make a good tent. She wasn't sure if she could drag it back to camp by herself. Perhaps Troy could help her. But he'd been injured, as well. And if she waited until morning, the other beasts might have devoured it.

She stood a moment, considering. She couldn't afford to let anything go to waste. She removed her belt and looped it around the creature's neck and started to pull. It was slow going, but eventually she dragged the carcass back to her camp.

Troy lay panting by the stream when she returned. He'd washed his wound, but he would need help bandaging it.

"Come here."

Troy jumped at the sound of her voice. Relief washed over him visibly when he saw her. His whole body relaxed and his face radiated warmth. "You're alive."

She nodded. "We need to get you sewn up."

She fashioned a spit over the fire and hung a pot from it to boil water. She didn't talk as she pulled out her supplies—bandages, a needle, thread, and herbs for a poultice. When the water boiled, she dipped a cloth in it and washed Troy's wound again.

You killed it." Troy winced as Rina sewed shut the gash in his middle. "How?"

"My blood. Somehow it hurt the thing, made it vulnerable to my sword."

"That doesn't make sense. It only wanted to kill me *more* when it tasted my blood. Why did yours hurt it?"

"I don't know."

"Was it the magic you used?"

Rina shook her head. "The magic didn't seem to affect it at all. And my blood also repelled another one that was nearby."

"Is your blood enchanted?"

Rina packed the herbs into the wound and wrapped bandages around Troy's middle. "Maybe. Whatever the reason, I think I know how to make our safe area."

Whirlwind

Rina sliced a knife across her palm and squeezed splatters of blood along the trail, drops every few feet on either side of the path. She could only hope it was enough to ward off the creatures and allow for safe passage through the forest to her camp.

It had worked around the campsite, at any rate. Creatures had come near, sniffed the outer edge, their violet eyes glowing in the dim light, then wandered away.

She and Troy had been hiding in the forest for two full weeks, safe, but Rina knew she couldn't stay ensconced in her hideaway forever. She began making the trail, a little more each day, so she and Troy could travel safely between the forest and the village.

As she walked along the path, she planned her coup against the king with Troy. "I need to get inside the castle. I need to get close to him, to gain his trust. Perhaps as a maid or a merchant."

"What if someone recognizes you?" Troy asked.

"Like who? The only time I've been near the castle was when I was little, and everyone who knows me is in the village. At least, without me there, everyone is safe."

"Are they? You haven't been there in two weeks. A lot can change in that amount of time."

She stepped closer to him. "It has been nice here, just the two of us."

Troy smiled and touched her cheek. They'd always been close friends, but hiding in the forest alone, sharing a shelter—their intimacy had deepened to a profound trust.

Though he'd never said anything, Rina knew he loved her. She loved him, too, but she couldn't be distracted by romance, not when there was so much at stake.

Somehow, she knew Troy understood. He'd never bring it up, not until she did first, but he knew her better than anyone ever had, and she knew he was content to be her rock, her tether, until she told him she was ready for more.

In the meantime, he would not let her rest easy.

He kissed her cheek. "Your people need you, Rina."

As much as he might also enjoy being away with her, he had said the same thing almost daily since they'd arrived in the forest.

"They know I haven't abandoned them."

"Do they?" Troy asked. "It's time to go back. Make a plan to get inside the castle, if you think that's your best route to the king, but you have to let the people know you're still fighting for them."

Rina sighed. "I'm more worried they've abandoned me."

Troy put an arm around her waist. "There's only one way to find out. It's time to go home."

Rina nodded and looked toward the edge of the forest.

Ahead, she could see light through thinning trees. Close enough that she could run that far without much risk of being eaten by a monster, but far enough that a casual observer wouldn't be able to see the trail head from the field.

She bandaged the cut on her hand, then set up a pillar of rocks as a guide for herself and Troy, to mark the entrance to the safe trail.

Taking a deep breath, she bolted the last few yards to the safety of open air beyond the forest's edge. She stopped in the field, panting. The trees looked so peaceful and inviting from this side, giving no hint of the horrors that lurked beneath their shadows. Looks could be so deceiving. Like the palace on the far hill. Its stone walls looked safe, a beacon of security, but inside, a raging dictator spewed forth his demands, enslaving the people, enforcing his will using a swarm of sorcerers.

When she'd caught her breath, Rina made a small stone marker so she'd know exactly where to enter the forest to reach her path. She pulled her hood up over her head and made her way to the village, ducking behind buildings and into alleys in order to be seen by as few people as possible, until she arrived at the tavern where her mother worked.

She slipped in the back.

The cook dropped his ladle in the pot of stew he was stirring. "Rina! We thought you was dead. Last we heard—"

"Shh!" Rina warned. "Is my mother here?"

"Aye. Waiting on a bunch of merchants."

"Guild?"

"Of course. No one else can get through the king's blockade."

Rina squeezed the cook's hand. "Please don't tell anyone you saw me. It's best if they believe I was eaten by monsters."

"Of course, child."

"Thank you." Rina pulled her hood a little lower and stepped out of the kitchen to the area behind the bar.

Her mother appeared a moment later, carrying a tray of empty tankards. She almost dropped it when she saw Rina.

Rina caught the tray and set it on the bar.

Her mother embraced her. "My girl. My sweet baby. I feared…" Her voice broke as she trailed off.

Rina held her as quiet sobs shook them both. "I'm fine. I have a safe place in the middle of the forest. Troy is with me."

"The monsters?"

"We found a way to keep them from attacking."

"How?"

"I can't explain now. I just wanted you to know I'm safe. How is everyone?"

"Do you remember Eli? The cooper's son? He was working in the king's stables, and sending us information every time new sorcerers came to the castle. The king found out about him. He was hanged four days ago, and the sorcerers scattered pieces of him on all four sides of the kingdom as a warning."

Rina shuddered. "And Shyla?"

"Still in the palace kitchen. She brings us news when she can. The latest is that the king seems to be amassing an army. We believe he plans to expand his rule beyond the borders of Legerdemain."

Rina felt as though an icy claw gripped her heart. The poverty, the famine, the fear that any perception of dissent would result in an unimaginable curse…

"I'm going to stop him. I won't let him take any more power than he already has."

"How can you?"

"I don't know. I'm still working on a plan. In the meantime—"

"Wench!" A voice from the far table hollered. "More ale!"

Margaret jumped. She grabbed a pitcher of ale. "I'll be right back."

Rina stepped back into a corner to wait.

"Pardon me, miss."

A man in a dark cloak stepped forward. A sorcerer. She could tell by the royal seal he wore around his neck.

Rina froze.

"Are you ill? I'm speaking to you."

She couldn't pretend she didn't see him. She smiled. "What can I do for you?"

"Ale."

Rina had helped Margaret often enough to bluff her way as a serving maid. She handed him a mug.

Their fingers brushed.

A jolt of something shot through her, some sort of magic passing between them.

Did he do something to her? Some sort of spell?

But he seemed as surprised as she was. He stepped backward, the hood of his cloak falling back, revealing his face.

Rina couldn't help but stare at him. He was older than she by a considerable margin, though still very handsome, but that wasn't why she couldn't draw her gaze from his face. Something in his eyes captured her, held her.

The world seemed to spin around them, a whirlwind of confusion, tossing reason and faith, anger and love, passion and death, into a mixed jumble of emotion and insanity, drawing them toward each other only to pull them apart. They stared at each other, just they two in the center of a swirling storm, at odds with each other and yet somehow in perfect harmony.

She knew he must be incredibly powerful to have this kind of effect over her. Years of caution, living under the king's dictatorship, and the devastating effects of defying him, told her she should kill the sorcerer right then, before he had a chance to do more harm, but she couldn't move.

Something jolted her, breaking the spell that kept her looking into the stranger's eyes.

It was her mother, yanking her arm, pulling her back toward the kitchen.

"What are you doing?" Margaret hissed.

Rina looked between Margaret and the door that swung closed, blotting out her view of the man.

"Go, now!" Margaret stuffed a loaf of bread and a chunk of dried meat into Rina's arms as she pushed her out the back door. "I'll leave more supplies for you under the tree where you and Troy used to play behind the cottage. Hurry! And pray he didn't recognize you!"

"Why? Who is he?"

Margaret brushed Rina's face with her fingertips, agony filing her eyes. "He is the king's head sorcerer."

Training

The blood-smeared knife sliced through the air and landed, *thunk*, right in the creature's eye.

"You have to show me how to do that," Rina said. "I'm good with a knife up-close, but I still can't throw it like that."

"It's in how you hold it." Troy retrieved the knife from the dead monster. He took her hand and placed a knife in it. "Like this."

Rina started to adjust her hold.

Troy laughed. "No. You always think your way is the best, but if you would just trust me for once, you'd see the difference."

Rina looked at him. "I do trust you."

He smiled. "Then do what I tell you." He stood behind her and held her arm. He rested his other hand on her hip, rotating it slightly. "Aim with your whole body. We're aiming for that tree trunk. Throw like this."

Rina threw. "I did it!"

"Good." Troy handed her another knife.

Last time she'd gone to the village, she'd traded for supplies. Game and vegetation were plentiful in the forest, where none but she could travel safely, so the blacksmith and the baker and others were happy to get fresh meat and berries and things in exchange for knives and blankets and other supplies.

"You're doing it again," Troy said.

"Doing what?"

"Changing the way you hold the knife."

"It's more comfortable this way."

Troy sighed. "I know, but you said yourself it's not as accurate. Do it the way I showed you."

The second throw was not as accurate as the first, but after several more tries, most of which at first bounced ineffectually off the tree trunk, she managed to consistently get it to stick in the tree, even if it wasn't quite where she was aiming.

"Take a break and help me move this thing," Troy said after awhile.

Together, they dragged the dead creature back to the camp. The creatures had so many different features, she found uses for most of them. Furry hides to trade in town, claws to use for knives, feathers to use for stuffing mattresses...

They'd found that the meat of the creatures was inedible, but the strong hides made exceptional roofs. Almost nothing went to waste.

"I'll take care of this," Troy said, indicating the carcass. "You keep practicing your throwing."

The next day, she and Troy practiced fencing. He'd taught her the basics years ago, when he first began training to be a soldier, so he'd have someone to practice with, and they'd worked together when she began planning her revolt, but Rina needed to hone her skills if she wanted to stand a chance against the king's forces.

Her arms burned and her legs nearly gave out, but she couldn't stop now.

"Again," she demanded every time Troy disarmed her or delivered what would be a killing blow. "Again."

"No. It's time for a break."

"I don't need a break," Rina insisted between gasps as she fought to catch her breath.

Troy stepped toward her and took her sword. He quietly walked both his sword and hers back to the shelter.

"Troy, come back. I need to learn this."

He emerged from the shelter and came to her. He slid his arms around her waist and looked at her. "You won't learn any faster by wearing yourself out. You need some rest. Besides, it's almost dusk. We need to build a fire and catch something to eat."

Rina sighed and leaned into him, enjoying the comfort of his arms around her. She let his embrace linger for a moment before pulling away. "You build the fire and I'll go get food."

She left Troy within the safety of the camp and its blood-lined border, took her bow, and wandered into the forest. She came upon a covey of quail and shot two before they managed to scurry to safety. At least there was one fighting skill she had mastered.

As she walked back toward the camp, a rabbit crossed her path, pausing to sniff the air. She stood still and carefully pulled a knife from her belt. Squaring her hips the way Troy showed her, holding the knife just so, she threw.

The knife struck the rabbit right in the neck.

By the time she reached the camp, she'd killed three more rabbits and two more quail with her knives, despite having missed twice as many more.

"What are all these for?" Troy asked. "We can't eat all of them, and they'll attract wild animals. The kinds that aren't going to be stopped by the blood barrier."

"We'll take them into town tomorrow and trade them. We need more knives. And swords. Whatever we can get. We have to start building an armory."

Troy took the animals from her without another word. He would follow her and support her, but she could see in his eyes he was beginning to question her, the longer she delayed.

The king was too strong, his sorcerers too powerful.

But his unspoken opinion was right. She had to move forward.

***

They walked to the village before dawn the next morning. Rina handed Troy two rabbits and a quail, keeping one of each. "Take those to the blacksmith and see how many knives he'll make for us in return.

I'm going to go see my mother. Meet me by the tree behind her house at noon."

Troy took an alley that led toward the back of the blacksmith's shop, and Rina walked around the outside of the village until she reached Margaret's house. She tapped softly at the back door.

Margaret opened it a crack, her face white, eyes wide with fear. She visibly relaxed when she saw Rina. "What are you doing here?"

"I brought you this." Rina held out the rabbit and the quail. "What's wrong?"

"Come in, quickly." Margaret glanced out the door, checking all around before closing it.

"Mother, what is going on?"

Margaret led Rina to the front room. The windows were covered and it was dark except for the glow of coals in the fireplace. A man lay on the hearth, his arm badly wounded, and a woman sat beside him, weeping softly.

Rina hurried to the man's side. "What happened?"

"The king's soldiers attacked him last night," Margaret said. "They accused him of plotting against the king because he refused to give them any more of his crops."

"We needed it to survive," the woman moaned. "Our children are practically starving as it is." She pointed to three young children asleep on a mat in the corner.

"They showed up just a few minutes ago. Someone told them I might be able to help."

Rina and Margaret worked quickly, washing and bandaging the man's wound.

"They'll be back," Margaret said softly. "The soldiers will come to take him to prison, and they'll take everything of value. Tarin and the children will starve. They need a place to hide."

Rina took a deep breath. There was only one solution. She hadn't wanted to drag anyone else into her vendetta, but the king was turning on his own people now. She had no other choice. "They'll have to come with me. To the forest."

The woman gasped. "You would sacrifice us to the creatures?"

"You'll be safe if you do as I say. It won't be easy. You'll all have to help care for the camp, and learn to use weapons to defend yourselves, but you'll be safe from the king's men."

Margaret drew Rina to the kitchen. "What are you thinking? These people are farmers, not soldiers. You can't expect them to start a war."

Rina looked at her mother. "The land is a barren wasteland. It has yielded all it can. People will soon begin to starve, and the king will slaughter them for not giving up what little they have. The only way to survive is to fight back. I don't expect them to begin the war. I expect them to fight in the war that has already begun."

Destiny

Rina pulled the last of the rope across the border of the camp.

Camp. It was more like a village than a camp, now. Refugees from the villages gathered at Margaret's house to be ushered to the safety of the forest whenever Rina or Troy came in for supplies.

Those trips were becoming sparser, however. The villages had fewer supplies, especially to provide for the ever-increasing population in the forest, and the more refugees they snuck from the villages, the greater the risk of detection. Rina had killed three sorcerers just in the last month because she saw them lurking near her mother's house and the tavern.

Her thoughts drifted to the one she'd seen in the tavern that day. The way his gaze pierced her, the feeling of the world falling away around them as they stood there, staring at one another. His dark eyes haunted her, invading her dreams and her thoughts.

She shook the memory away. There was work to be done, here and now.

The forest needed to be tamed. Wild beasts had lived there even before the sorcerers' abominations had taken up residence, and those were not deterred by Rina's blood.

Fire and noise kept all but the boldest away, but the men and women needed to be trained to protect themselves and the children.

The forest plants and wildlife had not been drained by overuse of magic, but the people had to learn which plants could be eaten, and how to gather enough, and how to cook over an open fire, and all the sorts of things that farmers and villagers never had reason to know.

The one blessing was, for the first time in years, everyone had enough to eat. Where the kingdom lay in ruins, crops withering and people trudging through muck just to harvest the barest amount of food needed to survive, the forest thrived. Except for the monsters that lurked just beyond the border, awaiting any who might stray beyond the trail of Rina's blood that marked the safe zone, the forest made an ideal place to live. Plants grew thickly in the untainted soil, and now, with all the extra hands, gardens were being cultivated and shelters were being erected.

Rina had begged her mother to come, but Margaret refused. "Your place is to lead those people, to begin taking this land back for them. My place is here, collecting information to help you so you can do your job and leading the people to safety."

One day she'd convince Margaret to come, but she would wait until it was a little safer.

Rina returned to her shelter at the center of the camp and bandaged her arm. The scars on her hands had been reopened so many times, she'd been forced to start cutting other areas to retrieve blood. Angry red lines crisscrossed her arms, but it was the only way to keep the ever-growing colony safe.

When she finished, she lay down to rest. Troy brought her soup, bread, and water. His presence beside her filled her with comfort. He was the only one she dared tell her thoughts to. "I don't know how long I can keep doing this."

"I know. But you have to, just a little longer."

She took his hand and squeezed. "You have helped me and supported me and been a better friend than I ever could've hoped for, but I can't keep on like this. I'm killing myself. And for what? A camp of weary people with no other home."

"This isn't just a community of outcasts. We're not here just to provide a haven for people trying to escape from William. This is an army. These are the people who will help you defeat the king."

"Why me? Why do I have to lead them? Why do I have to destroy the king? Surely there's a general or a sorcerer or...someone more suited to leading an uprising. Someone who doesn't have to bleed herself just to stay safe."

"Don't you see?" He stroked her face with his fingers. "There's a reason only you can keep the monsters away, a reason these people are willing to follow you."

She smiled weakly. "My mother said the same thing."

"Mistress Rina, pardon me," a voice at the entrance interrupted.

Rina sat up. "What is it?"

"Colin will not take his turn cleaning the latrines. He claims that is woman's work, and his duty is to help guard the camp."

Rina sighed. She gripped Troy's hand. "Help me up."

Leaning on Troy for support, she made her way to the source of the dispute. "What is the meaning of this?" she asked Colin, a man who boasted a few more years than she but wore the surly disposition of a spoiled child. He had come with the most recent group of refugees.

"I am not a servant or a woman. I was part of the king's royal guard. I will not do tasks that are beneath me."

"You *were*. You are not any more. Now you are here, and you will do as I say. If you choose not to follow the rules of my camp, you're welcome to leave. Give my regards to the creatures on the other side of my borders."

Colin gulped. Without another word, he took the shovel from the woman who'd reported him and trudged toward the latrine.

Troy pulled Rina close. "You're a good leader."

"It doesn't take a particularly wise or powerful general to yell at an unruly little boy."

Troy snorted. "True. But there's more to you than that."

"You say that like you know something I don't."

A frown crossed his face.

"Troy? What is it? What do you know?"

"Nothing. But I know there's more I don't know."

"Stop speaking in riddles. What are you talking about?"

"We should go see Margaret."

***

Under the cover of darkness, Rina and Troy made their way to Margaret's cottage.

"Stay here," Troy whispered. He left Rina by the tree out back and went to the door. He returned a moment later and gave her the all-clear signal.

Margaret embraced her as soon as she was inside. "This is a pleasant surprise. What brings you here?"

Rina sat at the table and took the cup of ale Margaret offered. "Troy said I needed to talk to you."

"Oh? Why is that?"

"I told him I didn't think I was qualified to lead an army."

"I see." A crease furrowed Margaret's brow.

"Mother, please. Tell me."

Margaret took her hand. "You know I've always loved you as my own child."

"Of course. I never questioned that."

Margaret nodded. "I also never pretended you were mine. I let people make whatever assumptions they wanted. I thought it the best way to keep you safe, if they thought you were an illegitimate waif, but I always told you the truth. Your mother died shortly after you were born and your care was entrusted to me. What I never told you, though, was who your parents really were."

Rina gulped. "What do you mean?"

"What do you know of the Revolution? The night the king took the throne?"

"King William believed the throne was rightfully his, so he made a pact with the sorcerers to help him claim it from his brother. In order to ensure the throne could never revert to his brother's line, he killed his brother and his newborn nephew."

Margaret nodded. "Yes. But something else happened that night, something only two people still living know. The baby boy King William killed was not the firstborn. The queen gave birth to another baby that night. A baby girl."

Rina sucked in her breath. "No."

"Yes, my daughter. You are the true king's child, the rightful heir to the throne."

Rina felt like the air was leaving the room, slowly suffocating. "It's not possible."

Her mother smiled gently. "Why do you think I never objected when you began this fight? Why do you think I helped you and encouraged you, rather than begging you to stay home and be safe? As much as it pains me to see you in danger, I know I can't keep you from your true calling."

"Why did you never tell me?"

Margaret took a deep breath. "It never seemed to be the right time. I didn't want to put too much pressure on you before you were ready. But now you are."

Troy squeezed her hand. "I knew there had to be something, some reason. That is why you are the only one who can defeat the monsters the king created."

Margaret nodded agreement. "People flock to follow you because, even though they don't realize it, they are *your* people. And that is why only you can lead them. Only you can overthrow the king and restore the kingdom. This is your destiny."

Attraction

"The girl who was here a few weeks ago, last time I was here, where is she?" Jarok asked.

He hadn't been able to stop thinking about her. She haunted his dreams and distracted his thoughts until he could hardly focus on anything else. Eventually, he realized the only cure was to try to find her.

The maid behind the bar quivered, her aging face white as she stared up at him. "I can't imagine who you mean, sir."

Of course, she was lying. She was the same one who'd hurried the girl away when he came in that night. He could make the woman talk, force her to tell him where—and who—the girl was, but decided against it. It would do him no good to find the girl if he'd terrorized her friends. "Do you have parchment and a pen?"

The woman nodded and disappeared, returning a moment later with a quill, a jar of ink, and a scrap of parchment.

Jarok quickly scratched a note. *Tomorrow night, midnight, the tree by the well on the south side of the village.* He blew on the ink to dry it, folded the parchment, and handed it to the barmaid. "If you happen to see her, give her this."

Jarok considered waiting and following the barmaid to try to find the girl but refrained. He wanted to meet the girl, not scare her away for good. He returned to the palace.

Ada was in the throne room when he arrived. Seeing him, her head cocked to one side and her brow furrowed.

"What is it?" Jarok asked.

"Something dangerous is on your horizon. The path you are on will lead to destruction."

"What path?"

"I cannot see it clearly. All I see is a woman. You are linked to her somehow, but she will lead you to your doom."

A woman. It couldn't be. Yet he couldn't deny the obvious. The girl from the tavern—he was drawn to her, connected in a way he couldn't comprehend, let alone explain. But she was a simple tavern maid. How could she lead to his doom? The only way he could hope to uncover that mystery was to follow through with the meeting.

***

The girl was sitting on the edge of the well when Jarok arrived the next night.

She looked the same as she did in his imagination, replaying over and over their brief encounter, the way her dark hair waved around her face and her lips looked like they were begging to be kissed.

Her eyes lit up and a smile teased the corners of her mouth when she saw him. She stood and took a step toward him, then stopped, shifting her feet awkwardly. "I got your note. Why did you want to see me?"

"I don't know, exactly. I just knew I had to see you again."

The smile that spread across her face was radiant. "You felt it, too."

He stepped forward and took her hand. A jolt shot through him, warming him. The air felt charged with energy, colors swirled in his vision. This was real. This was destiny. How or why she was connected to him he didn't know, but he knew it was real. This feeling, it was right. It was meant to be. Magic more powerful than any he could control had drawn them together.

He pulled her close and kissed her. She melted into his arms, so close he could feel her heart pounding in time with his own.

After a moment, she pulled away. "What is happening?"

"I don't know. I just know we're connected somehow."

"Is it magic?"

"It must be, although I've never worked with anything like this."

"Of course not, you're too busy creating monsters and things that destroy."

Her tone was harsh, bitter, and her eyes flashed with something akin to hate. The look was gone so quickly he almost thought he'd imagined it. She smiled up at him. "What I mean is, this is beautiful, what is happening between us. It's different from the king's magic."

The thought struck something in him. He'd been doing the king's bidding for so long, he scarcely remembered that there was more magic in the world. She was right. What would it be like to control the kind of pure, blissful magic he felt when he was near her? If he could live his life with this feeling…

Ada's warning sprang to his consciousness. He pushed the thought away. Looking into this girl's pure, innocent eyes, feeling the warmth that radiated around him when he was near her, he could not believe she could lead to his doom. She was his destiny.

He kissed her again. She pulled away. "I should go."

"Let me walk you home. It's not safe out here, with the rebels wantonly attacking."

And amused twinkle sparkled in her eyes. "You're the head of the king's sorcerers. You're more frightening than any villager or rebel, and yet I'm here with you."

"You're safe with me."

She smiled. "I know. But don't worry, I can take care of myself. You should worry about getting yourself home safely. There's an assassin killing sorcerers lurking about. For all you know, it could be me."

Jarok chuckled. "I trust you." He stroked her face with his fingertips. "When can I see you again?"

"Two days from now. Here, at the same time."

He gave her a final kiss. "Until then."

He thought about her, her smile, the magic that radiated between them, her soft lips, every moment that he'd been with her, short though it had been. He'd never thought he could be in love. Working for the king had left little time for romance, but this girl—he couldn't put his finger on why, but neither could he let her go.

Perhaps he should ask Ada for something more specific. Perhaps there was a way to counter whatever dire fate she foresaw.

He had to try. Seeing the girl again didn't sate his desire for her, it only made it stronger.

It wasn't until he reached his room at the palace that he realized he didn't even know her name.

Romance

Rina ran all the way back to the camp in the forest. She threw her arms around Troy and kissed him, full on the mouth.

Troy stepped back, eyes wide, and sputtered. "Rina, what?"

"I found it. My way in."

"Way into what?"

"The castle. I know how to get close to the king."

Troy's face broke into a smile. "How? What is it?"

"The king's head sorcerer."

The smile immediately fell from Troy's face. "You cannot be serious."

She laughed and patted his cheek. "Don't you see? This is what we've been looking for. A way to get close to the king. If I can gain the sorcerer's trust, I can discover how to destroy the king."

"So you're just going to march into the castle and ask the king's head sorcerer to tell you everything he knows?"

Rina laughed again. How could he know what she meant? Dear, sweet, protective Troy. "No, I already met him. I saw him once at the tavern, and then he wanted to meet me. I saw him tonight. I think He cares for me. I can use that against him."

"You…Rina, are you out of your mind? It's clearly a trap. He's doing the same thing to you that you're trying to do to him."

Rina shook her head. "He doesn't know who I am."

Troy didn't look convinced. "How can you know that?"

"I can just tell. To him, I'm just a pretty face."

"And how do you know he's not telling someone the same thing about you?"

Rina frowned. Why did he not understand the importance of this? "Well, I have to do something. You're the one who keeps reminding me I can't hide forever. I have to move forward, and this is the missing piece of my plan."

He shook his head. "I don't like it."

She squeezed his hands. "I can do this, Troy. I *must* do this."

Troy pulled her close. "When do you see him again?"

"Tomorrow."

"Be careful."

"I will," she promised.

***

Rina's heart thudded in her chest as she waited by the well for the sorcerer. She started to tell herself not to be nervous, then realized she wasn't.

She was…excited.

She was actually looking forward to seeing him, and not just because of what she could learn from him. She wanted to see him because of how he made her feel.

She felt him as soon as he turned the corner and came into view, that magic pulling them together, sparking with life.

His cloak billowed around him, making him look regal.

She stood and took a step toward him.

"You came," he said.

"Of course," she smiled. "Did you think I wouldn't?"

He pulled her into his arms. "I scarcely dared hope. You are so beautiful."

Rina's cheeks felt hot and her hands trembled. "I'm sure there are plenty of pretty girls in the palace."

"Perhaps. I've never noticed."

Rina opened her mouth, but couldn't think of anything to say.

"Shall we go for a walk?" the sorcerer asked.

"Yes, let's," Rina agreed quickly.

The sorcerer took her hand and intertwined his fingers with hers.

Even the feel of his hand felt different than Troy's. Firmer, more possessive.

He led her down the main street toward the road to the West Village. They didn't go far, just meandered slowly up and down through the village.

They walked in silence for a little while. Rina could hardly believe how just the feel of her hand in his gave her a thrill like none she'd ever experienced. The magnetism that drew her to him only seemed to grow stronger with every meeting.

"Do you know," the sorcerer said after a little while, "I feel as though I've known you forever, and yet I don't even know your name."

A wave of panic jolted through her. Of course, she couldn't give her real name. "Oh, I...ah...Alise."

Margaret had once told her that if she'd ever had another daughter, she would have been named Alise. It was the first name that came to Rina's mind.

"Alise. A beautiful name. It suits you. I am Jarok."

"Jarok." It felt good on her tongue, strong and masculine, powerful, yet tender.

"I like the way my name sounds when you say it," Jarok said.

"Likewise," Rina smiled.

"Alise. And you work in the tavern."

"Oh, I...I do a little of a lot of things."

"Such as?"

Rina shrugged. "I do whatever is needed. But that is dull. Tell me, what is it like to be a sorcerer? To have the ability to wield magic?"

"The feel of harnessing the earth's energies, letting them flow through you—there's nothing like it in the world Although lately, the energy seems to be waning."

"Like it's all been used up?'

Jarok looked at her sideways. "Who told you that?"

96

Rina gulped. He made her feel so at ease, she'd almost let slip too much. "I heard a rumor once, years ago, that too much magic strips the land. I'm sure it was nothing. A bitter old man started it, angry that his crops were failing."

Jarok grunted. "We still have plenty of magic to work with."

"Good. Else how would you protect the kingdom?"

Jarok smiled, warming her with the intensity of his gaze. "Precisely. The kingdom is my priority, second only to the king himself. The magic that I have put around him to protect him makes him nigh invulnerable."

"What a relief." It took all the subterfuge Rina could muster to give enthusiasm to her words.

They walked and talked well into the night, mostly about little things. Jarok told her of his life as a young boy who could wield magic in a land where such abilities were frowned upon, and how the king's trust in him had empowered him to become one of the most powerful sorcerers anyone had heard of, at least in the surrounding regions.

Had it been any other king, any other kingdom, Rina would have felt great pride for him in such an accomplishment, but how could she applaud him when his power came at the hands of a tyrant and at the expense of her land?

She glanced at the sky. It was late. Troy would be worried.

"I should go," she said.

"Already?" Jarok asked.

"We've been walking for hours."

Jarok sighed. "I suppose we have. Time has so little meaning when I'm near you."

Rina smiled. "I feel the same. But my…family will be worried."

Jarok nodded. "Very well. May I walk you home?"

"Just to the tavern, please."

He nodded and walked slowly in that direction. "When may I see

97

you again?"

"When would you like to?"

"I would like to never stop, but I suppose I can wait until tomorrow."

Rina giggled. "Tomorrow it is, then. By the well?"

"Yes." Jarok paused outside the tavern door. He gathered Rina into his arms and kissed her, slowly, deeply, thoroughly.

Rina kissed him back, warring with herself, struggling to remember that the only reason she agreed to see him, the only reason she let him kiss her like that, was to gain his trust so she could kill the king.

That was the same thing she told herself every night for the next week as she continued to meet him.

Tryst

"Where were you?"

Rina turned. Troy stood in the door of their shelter, now improved so it was almost a little hut, his eyes accusing.

"I was gathering information."

"You were meeting *him* again."

Rina tossed her head. "What I do is my business. I'm working to free my people, and I will do whatever it takes to accomplish that end, even meeting with the king's head sorcerer."

Troy stepped to her side and took her hand. "You can't trust him. He is loyal to the king. He will betray you."

Guilt stabbed through her. Troy, her friend, her love, who had waited patiently, supporting her every decision, now had to wait at home alone while she let her enemy court her so she could gain his trust.

Rina sighed. "I haven't told him anything. He believes I'm nothing more than a simple maiden named Alise he met in town one day. There is nothing for him to betray."

"What if he follows you? If he sees you go into the forest he'll know who you are."

"I'm careful not to let him see me leave." She held his hand. If only she could explain so he would understand. "I can't afford not to meet him. Our spies in the castle are being killed, one by one. I can't put any more of them in danger. This is my best chance of finding the king's weakness."

"How will you do that? Do you really think he gives up the king's secrets to every pretty face?"

"I've been invited to dine with him tomorrow night. While I'm in the palace, I'll find a way to make new contacts. At some point, someone will be able to tell me about the magic that protects the king."

99

"I wish you wouldn't go. It's too dangerous."

Rina squeezed his hand. "I cannot lead an army where I am not willing to go myself, and I will not lead them into a situation for which we are unprepared."

Troy pulled her into his arms. His mouth hovered near hers. "That's not the only danger I'm worried about."

Rina lifted up on her toes and met his lips with hers.

Kissing him was so different from kissing Jarok. With Jarok, there was magnetism and excitement, the thrill of danger. Troy was steady and pure, the depth of his love reflecting in everything he did, even the way he cautiously pulled her closer, kissed her more deeply.

After a few moments, she pushed him back. "You know how much I care for you, how much I depend on you. But you have to trust that I can take care of myself."

He exhaled heavily. "I'll care for the camp until you return."

***

Rina went to her mother's house early in the morning. She bathed and dressed in her finest gown, and brushed her hair until it shone.

She borrowed a horse from the blacksmith in the village, and early in the evening she arrived at the formidable castle wall.

She knocked at the guardhouse door. "My name is Alise. Jarok is expecting me."

The guard allowed her in and led her down a series of opulent hallways. The poverty and stench that permeated the city and villages on the other side of the thick stone walls seemed worlds away.

Rina's stomach turned. What kind of ruler could hide in the pristine confines of the palace while his people starved and rotted away with disease? When she was queen…

No, it did no good to think like that. She must take it one step at a time. First, she must find a way to bring the king down.

"Alise. I'm so glad you could come."

Rina held out her hand. Jarok's dark eyes burned into hers as he lifted her hand to kiss her fingers. Her breath caught as heat sparked through her at his touch.

Her thoughts went back to Troy, who waited for her back at the camp. She was doing this for him, for all of them. This moment was not hers to enjoy.

If only the rapid beating of her heart knew that.

Her voice came out as scarcely more than a whisper. "I am pleased to be here."

He led her to a table laden with delicacies.

Bile rose in her throat. "Where did you get all this? The farms are not producing this quality of food."

"No, they aren't. The king has food for the palace imported."

Rina fought to keep a smile on her face as she tasted the rich concoctions spread out before her. Her people in the forest ate better than anyone in the villages, but even they hadn't had anything even remotely like this in more than twenty years. Rich, buttery breads, seasoned meats, salads with all types of vegetables and fruits.

"Try this." Jarok handed her a bite of some sort of seasoned meat wrapped in soft, flaky dough.

It tasted like bark to Rina. "If the king has access to this kind of cuisine, why does he not feed his people better?"

"The rebels in the forest make it impossible to bring more than what is needed for the palace through their blockade."

Rina burned at the accusation. To insinuate *she* had anything to do with the country's poverty! She forced her voice to remain calm. "The farms were on the decline long before the rebels existed. My mother says they stopped producing years ago."

Jarok waved his hand dismissively. "At any rate, the king has a plan to fix things."

"Oh?"

"He's going to expand the trade route by conquering neighboring lands."

"And you think that will solve the country's problems?"

"Why wouldn't it? More trade means more food, and more sustenance for the people here."

Rina bit her tongue to keep from giving herself away. How could she ever have thought this man handsome?

She gulped down her anger before responding. "Don't you worry that instead of bringing us prosperity it might bring poverty to the lands that are conquered?"

"Why should it?"

Rina choked. She could be still no longer. "Because it is the constant use of magic that is sucking the life out of this land! How can you use power so freely with so little regard for its consequences? The king brought you and the others like you here, and you have destroyed our land."

Jarok stood, towering over her. "And what if we did? This is not my land. I don't care what happens here."

Rina shoved away from the table and faced him. "Fool. Do you think the king will ever let you leave? You are his slave as much as any of the peasants in the villages. This is your land now, whether you were born here or not. You will die in misery with the rest of us if you continue to serve the king. And you'll be the first one I—"

Her threat cut off as Jarok's mouth covered hers. He pulled her against him, kissing her deeply.

Fire raged in her blood, hate turning quickly to lust, without her intention or consent.

She melted against him, returning the kiss with equal passion.

Breathless, she pulled away from him "I have to go. My people need me."

She ran from the castle, almost knocking over an old lady in the hall in her hurry.

She hadn't found the king's weakness, and she'd exposed her true purpose to the king's most trusted advisor. She very likely had just ruined everything.

Then again, if she played it right, she might just have found a way to win.

Subterfuge

"You're going to him again? Even after everything he said?" Troy asked.

Rina fastened her cloak. "I have to. I need to know more." She didn't mention the gnawing desire eating away at her, demanding to be with him, needing to see him one more time.

"How do you know he believed your apology? What if it's a trap?"

"He believed me."

"And if he didn't?"

"Then I'll kill him. I've killed plenty of sorcerers. He will be no different."

"He's not just any sorcerer. He's the king's *head* sorcerer. He's been working for the king since before you were born."

Rina stood on her toes and kissed his cheek. "Trust me. I have to go. I'll be back by morning."

She hurried from the camp toward the village.

The stables were deserted except for the soft sounds of animals shuffling in their stalls. The grooms were likely enjoying the company of the tavern maids over a cold ale.

Rina scampered up the ladder to the loft to wait.

A short while later, he arrived. He stood in the doorway for a few moments. "Hello?" he called softly.

"Up here," Rina said.

She felt for her knife, its hard blade reassuring her, just in case Troy was right and it was a trap.

Jarok climbed the ladder, not even seeming to worry whether she would attack him while she had the advantage. And why would he? Even before he got to the top of the ladder, her skin began to tingle, his nearness intoxicating her. How could he make her feel that way? She didn't love him, not like she loved Troy, and yet she did. She was tempted to trust him completely, despite all she knew.

Was that why he came? Did he trust her because of their connection, throwing out all logic and reasoning?

He sprang to the top and wrapped his arms around her, burying his face in her neck. "I was so happy to get your message. I worried I'd not be able to make amends for angering you."

"No, I was rash. How could you know my thoughts?"

Jarok kissed her. "You were right. I don't know how the people suffer when I live on the king's indulgence. But you also do not understand. I am at the mercy of the king. I serve him because I have no other choice."

Rina sat down and patted the soft hay beside her, inviting him to join her. "Why? Why can you not choose your own path?"

"I chose my path a long time ago. I bound myself to the king using very powerful magic."

"Any spell can be broken."

"Perhaps. But I cannot break it. The king's amulet holds magic older and more powerful than mine." Jarok stopped, pulling away slightly.

Did he know how much he'd just given away? She couldn't let him know just how important that information was to her.

Rina nestled in against his chest and kissed his neck. "Surely you're still free to choose some of you actions? After all, you're here with me."

He chuckled and kissed her again, running his hands down her arms and encircling her waist. "If only it were that simple. I can't intentionally do anything that would undermine the king's rule."

Rina kissed him, savoring his taste as much as she savored the realization that as long as she kept him close, he would continue to tell her what she needed to hear.

Troy's face pushed its way into her mind, his soulful eyes begging her not to go, his steady comfort supporting her all these months.

Jarok's hands caressing her pushed all thoughts of Troy away, and she surrendered to his touch.

"The king would not be pleased with me for shirking my duties to be here with you. As long as the king has the amulet, I am his."

Rina lay back in the hay and pulled him down with her, murmuring between her kisses, "Well, you're not his tonight."

Espionage

"That's Maralen," Margaret said. "She's a servant in the palace kitchens."

Rina looked across the busy tavern to where the young woman sat, her fingers toying with the handle of her mug. "Did she come to you or did you find her?"

"She came to me."

"How did she know how to find you? How do we know she can be trusted?"

"She is the daughter of a man named Oliver in your camp."

Rina nodded. "I know Oliver. Troy helped him escape when the king's men were coming for him."

Rina made her way through the crowd and sat opposite Maralen. Margaret followed and stood near, half listening, half watching for those who might try to eavesdrop on Rina and Maralen.

"I understand you have information for me," Rina said.

The woman nodded. "I serve the sorcerers, and I overheard them talking about the next supply train that will be coming into Legerdemain."

Rina leaned forward. "You know when it is coming?"

Maralen nodded. "A convoy of sorcerers is to meet it in two days time on the other side of the forest to escort it back through."

"Thank you, Maralen. You will be rewarded for your help. Do you have any other news to tell me?"

"Not yet. I'll contact her when I have anything else." Maralen nodded toward Margaret.

"Good. And what of the sorcerers who will be coming for the supply train? Will Jarok be with them?" Rina hoped Maralen didn't hear the slight hitch to her voice when she said Jarok's name.

If she did, she made no show of it. "No. He's too important. The king wouldn't risk him for a supply train."

Rina's heart stuttered. Good. She didn't want to worry about facing him. She couldn't focus on her mission if he were there. "Thank you, Maralen. You have been very helpful."

***

Rina waited by the side of the road, just inside the line of the trees. Her arm stung from the open wound that ran up it, but she needed the fresh scent of her blood to repel the creatures.

A small group of her followers stood close by, within the protective aura of her blood. They all held knives ready.

Down the road, the sound of hooves echoed. "Get ready," Rina whispered. "The more of them we kill now, the fewer will be able to protect the supply train."

A few moments later, a troop of sorcerers rounded the bend, riding hard.

"Now!" Rina shouted. She threw a knife, then a second, and a third before the sorcerers huddled together and formed a protective barrier around themselves. The air glowed with an eerie red light.

Rina threw another knife. It bounced off the barrier as if it had been stone.

"Get back," she told her followers. She crouched behind a rock, waiting for the spells that must inevitably come their way.

The sorcerers kept going, inching along the road, safe from her knives, but making no move to attack.

Maybe they couldn't. Maybe spells couldn't get out any more than knives could get in. Or perhaps, keeping the barrier up took all their concentration, leaving no room for another spell. wall as strong as stone to keep any knives from touching them.

Six of the ten sorcerers had fallen from their horses. Two were dead and the other four badly wounded. One managed to get to his feet

108

and hobble toward the circle of sorcerers that walked on down the road. He bounced against the barrier. "Let me in!" he shrieked.

Rina readied her knife, waiting to kill more of them, but when it became clear the sorcerers would not lower their barrier to let him in, she threw it at the limping sorcerer. "Help me pull their bodies into the forest," she ordered. "Let the creatures get a taste for sorcerer blood."

She retrieved her knives and began dragging the first body toward the forest. One of the still-living sorcerers feebly attempted to cast a spell her direction, but before he finished, a knife lodged in his throat and he collapsed to the ground.

Rina looked up.

Troy.

She smiled at him as he helped her drag the body into the forest.

As soon as Rina was a few feet away, two creatures emerged and began devouring the corpses. The rest of Rina's group stayed in the center of the road, out of range of the monsters, their knives trained on the slowly departing remaining sorcerers, in case they let the barrier fall while Rina was occupied disposing of the bodies.

She and Troy had almost finished depositing the last of the dead and wounded soldiers in the forest when Rina stopped. "Shh!"

She stood and looked down the road.

Hooves. Lots of them. Coming fast.

It was a trap. They'd been betrayed.

"Retreat!" she screamed. She grabbed Troy's hand and ran toward the edge of the forest.

Too late. An army, both soldiers and sorcerers, thundered around the bend. Sorcerers hurled spells, and soldiers hurled spears.

In moments, half of Rina's force lay writhing on the ground. She urged the survivors toward her, toward the safety of the forest and her protective blood.

She looked back toward the army one last time before

109

disappearing into the forest.

The leader of the king's forces, the one who led the charge, sat still atop his horse, staring after her. Their eyes locked.

Jarok.

The True Heir

Jarok slammed the door to his chambers and threw the first thing he laid his hands on, a clay goblet. It shattered against the far wall, the pieces raining down in shards and dust on the floor.

How could he have been so stupid? How much had he told her when he held her in his arms, so drugged by her presence he couldn't think straight? She'd gotten so upset the night he invited her for dinner. He should've known then she wasn't who he thought she was. Should've known better than to meet her again.

But he met her anyway. He talked for hours, giving away secrets of the sorcerers, details about the palace and the guards, sharing the most intimate knowledge with her, only to discover she was one of the rebels. Fairly high-ranking among them, too, judging by the way they followed her lead in the skirmish.

How had he managed to let so much slip without her revealing any of herself to him? Had she been a spy the whole time?

He had a hard time believing that. The magic between them was too powerful. Unless that was the whole point. Had she bewitched him? What power did she have over him that blinded him to her true purpose in meeting him night after night?

A harsh knock interrupted his thoughts.

The door opened and a young pageboy poked his head in. "The king wishes to see you immediately."

Jarok stalked to the throne room, working to compose himself along the way. The king couldn't possibly know about the girl, could he? Jarok hoped he'd never find out, but at least he had to make sure he could put his own story together, first. Perhaps he'd claim he was spying on the rebels, not the other way around.

He bowed upon entering the throne room. "You wanted to see

me, Your Majesty?"

Ada stood in the corner, eyeing him, a knowing look in her eyes. He shuddered. He hated not knowing how much the old crone saw in those visions of hers.

"The reports say this morning's campaign was a success," the king said.

"In a manner of speaking. We lost several sorcerers, but we routed the rebels. Our spy did her work well. The rebels had no idea it was a trap."

"And the supply train?"

"The troops went to escort it in. The rebels are wounded and disoriented. We don't expect any trouble from them. The supplies should arrive on schedule."

The king rubbed his hands together. "Excellent. Why do you not seem more pleased?"

Jarok forced a smile. "I am, Majesty."

"And the spy?"

"What of her?"

"The rebels will know who betrayed them," the king said. "She is of no more use to us."

Ada stepped forward. "If I may, Your Majesty."

The king nodded.

"It will serve us better to give the girl her reward. Although she may be useless now, there are others who will be encouraged to do the same if they see the benefit she has received for her loyalty."

The king rubbed his chin. "Very well. Summon her."

Jarok regarded Ada. She was wise. Her plan would be useful. They would need good spies, especially since Alise, or whatever her real name was, now had thorough details of the king's forces, thanks to him.

A servant scurried out and returned a few moments later with the serving girl, Maralen.

112

She bowed before the throne.

"Rise," the king said. He handed her a scroll and a bag of gold. "You have done well. Our campaign was successful, thanks to the information you fed the rebels. Here is the gold you were promised and your father's pardon. As soon as you can get word to him, he is free to return home."

Maralen curtsied deeply, tears filling her eyes. "Thank you, Majesty, thank you!"

Her fawning was cut off by the door to the throne room slamming open.

A soldier burst in, panting, his face red. He carried a large crate and a letter rolled into a scroll. "This was just delivered. I was told to give it to you personally, Your Majesty, and urgently."

The king nodded to Jarok.

Jarok opened the scroll and read aloud. "Declaration of War against William the Usurper."

That was all.

"Open the crate," the king ordered.

Jarok pried the lid off. He stumbled backward, gagging at the sight.

Inside was a severed head.

Lifeless eyes stared up at him.

The serving girl, Maralen, peeked over his shoulder. She began to scream, her high-pitched wails echoing off the stone walls. "Father!"

Another scroll was rolled up and tucked into the crate by the head. Jarok pulled it out and gingerly unrolled it. Blood dripped from the parchment onto his quivering hands as he read. "Such is the fate of any found guilty of treason against the rightful monarch, the legitimate ruler, the True Heir of Legerdemain."

Silence as thick as the congealed blood that covered Jarok's hands permeated the room.

Ada's eyes rolled back in her head and she collapsed to the floor, her body writhing in violent spasms. Her voice rose, high and ethereal, filling the room, "The Heir is the destruction of us all. Beware the True Heir!"

Loyalty

"Find her. Find anyone who knows her. She'll lead us to the enemies of the crown."

Jarok bowed low before the raging king. "Yes, your majesty. I know where to start looking."

He found the captain of the guard. "There's a tavern in the South Village. The wench who tends the bar knows her. Golden hair, nearing her middle years. Bring her to me."

There were several barmaids who worked at the tavern, it seemed. The king's guards returned with four women who fit the description Jarok gave. It didn't matter. He recognized her immediately. The woman who'd tried to keep him away from Alise, or whatever her real name was. "Her. Bring her to me. The others may go."

The guards followed him, escorting the wench, down to the dungeon where they shoved her into an iron chair.

Jarok stood before her, hands behind his back, towering over her. "Do you know why you're here?"

Her chin quivered, and a flash of understanding sparked in her eyes. "N-no."

Jarok smiled. "But you have an idea."

She shook her head. "I don't."

He decided to play along. "There's a girl who visits your tavern. She can't be more than twenty. I need to know where to find her."

"There are many young women who visit the tavern."

"You know the one I mean. You delivered a note to her for me once, don't you remember?"

Tears glistened in the woman's eyes, but she lifted her chin bravely. "I don't remember."

"I have reason to believe she is an enemy of the crown. If you do not help me, you will be found guilty of treason."

"So be it. I cannot help you."

Jarok rubbed his chin. Perhaps a different tactic. He dismissed the guards and pulled a chair close so he could sit at her level, as a confidant, rather than an interrogator. "Madam, you know more than you're telling me. If you're as close to her as I believe you are, you know how much we mean to each other. The king is looking for her. Believe me, he will find her, and as I'm sure you are aware, he is not a very forgiving man. Better if I find her first so I can protect her from his wrath."

"If you mean so much to her, why don't you know where she is?"

He smiled. "You already know the answer to that. But it doesn't mean I don't care about her. I swear to you, if you tell me where she is, I will keep her safe."

"I'm sorry. I do not know."

"But you can get a message to her. Tell her to surrender to me before it's too late."

A solitary tear made a track down the woman's cheek. "I can't do that."

"Why not? What hold does she have over you? I can keep you safe if she's threatening you. Just send her a message."

The wench laughed. "You fool. You have no idea what you're saying. I'm not protecting her because I'm afraid of her. She's my daughter. You'll never convince me to betray her."

"I can torture you. Conjure a spell to force you to tell me the truth."

"You'd better get started, then."

Jarok shoved his chair away and called the guards in. "Put her in a cell." He stomped to his chamber and began mixing ingredients together. A truth spell was incredibly complex. If it didn't kill the subject, it caused extreme pain as it manipulated the mind into giving up its secrets, and even then it might not be powerful enough to make a woman give up her own daughter.

Several hours later, the potion was complete. Jarok made his way down to the dungeon and opened up the cell.

The woman's body dangled from the ceiling, suspended from the rafters by strips of cloth torn from her petticoat.

Jarok cursed and threw the potion against the wall. He yelled for the guards. "Cut her down. Hang her body in the square and tell everyone the same thing will happen to anyone who protects the girl."

Turning Point

Hushed whispers and furtive glances greeted Rina when she walked into the tavern from the back entrance. "What is it?" she asked.

The cooks turned away, pained looks in their eyes.

"What is going on? What happened?

The tavern keeper bustled in. "This way." He led her around the building to the town square.

Rina fell to her knees, retching. "Why?" she managed to ask.

"They're looking for you. The king's head sorcerer sent for Margaret. Rumor is he tortured her before hanging her, trying to get information on how to find you."

"His head sorcerer? Are you sure?"

The tavern keeper nodded. "Completely. He came himself to watch the guards string her up. He said this would happen to anyone who helps you or protects you. Out of respect for Margaret, I won't turn you in, but you understand I can't have you come back to the tavern anymore."

Rina nodded. "I won't endanger anyone who is unwilling. You're sure it was the head sorcerer who did this?"

"I am certain. He gathered up several of my girls and when he identified Margaret, he sent the others home."

She could hardly believe Jarok killed her mother. How could he? How could she have fallen for someone who could do such a thing? She swiped a hand across her face, brushing away the tears. "Can you cut her down for me?"

He nodded and beckoned toward two stable boys who loitered nearby. Rina handed the tavern keeper a bag of coins, spoils from the last sorcerer she'd killed. "See that she's properly buried."

The tavern keeper nodded.

Rina went to the center of the square and rang the huge gong that hung there, the deep tones echoing all over the village.

People came out of shops and homes to see what the commotion was.

Rina stood on the base of the gallows so she could see out over the crowd. "The king and his sorcerer murdered my mother. I'm done hiding from him, done sneaking around. I'm going to fight back. Anyone who wants to join me, meet me at the edge of the forest directly south of here at sundown."

She hopped down and approached the tavern keeper. "I need a horse."

One of the stable boys went running, returning a few moments later with a horse. She tipped him well and promised to return the horse by evening.

Taking the left fork heading out of town, she rode hard until she reached the East Village. She repeated her message there, calling the people to join her forces, then rode on, circling the kingdom, traveling to the Four Villages and recruiting her army.

***

Shortly before sundown, she made her way back around to where she'd started. She sent the horse into the center of the village, trusting he'd make his way back to the stable, to his stall and food, and she made her way back toward the forest.

A small crowd waited for her there, mostly young men, farmers' sons and boys looking for adventure.

She greeted them cordially. "Thank you all for coming. Your lives are about to change. As of this moment, your allegiance belongs to me. If any of you are unsure of this cause, leave now. If you choose to stay you will swear to me your fealty, and you will demonstrate your loyalty by following me into the forest."

The first young man bowed before her and took her and. "I swear

119

to be loyal, faithful, and obedient to your rule."

He stood. "Lead the way, my lady."

One by one, they knelt before her and pledged themselves to her.

It was late into the night by the time she led them into the forest. "Stay near me and you'll be safe," she promised.

She sliced a cut in her arm and dabbed blood on each of them before leading them toward the camp.

Glowing amethyst eyes glared at them from the shadows, but Rina led on, her troupe following closely behind.

When they got to the camp, Rina sent the new recruits to bunk with others until new shelters could be built.

It was nearly dawn by the time everyone was sorted out.

Rina sat on a rock at the edge of the camp and finally allowed herself to weep, grieving not only for the loss of her mother but also for the loss of her lover.

What kind of twisted spell had drawn her into his arms, only to have him betray her? Somehow, a part of her thought he would defect. That he'd realize the injustice of the king and agree to help her. How could he not, if he loved her as much as he said?

And how could she love him, when he turned on her so violently? Only a few nights before, he'd held her in his arms and told her he'd do anything for her, and today, he'd killed her mother.

He was as evil as the king he served and she was a fool. All along, she'd had someone who loved her completely, and she spat on that for the sake of fleeting passion.

Just as the sun began filtering through the trees, she finally made her way back to her hut.

Vows

Rina stumbled into her hut, eyes blurred by tears, scarcely able to walk. After everything, he'd still betrayed her. She thought she meant something to him, thought somehow she'd change his mind, that he would leave the king's service and join her, but as soon as he'd gotten what he wanted from her, he turned on her.

She tried to muffle her sobs, but it didn't matter. Troy was awake, pacing the hut. He pulled her into his arms when he saw her, holding her tightly. "What happened? Where were you?"

"I went to see Jarok. He told me…it doesn't matter. He lied. He betrayed me."

She fell against his chest, letting loose all the hurt, letting the strength of his arms comfort her. He held her until the sobs subsided, then gently lifted her face and cupped it in his hands.

She looked up at him, saw the depth of love in his eyes. How had she not noticed before? All the torrid passion of her feelings for Jarok that ended in pain, when all the while Troy waited with undying loyalty.

She raised up on her toes and kissed him.

He pulled away for a moment, shock written on his features, then leaned down and pressed his mouth to hers, hungrily, desperately.

She returned the kiss, needing his steadfast devotion more than she knew was possible.

After a long moment, she pulled away and looked into his eyes. "Marry me."

Troy's eyebrows furrowed together. "What?"

"I want to marry you, Troy. I didn't even realize it until now, but you're the only one I want."

Troy frowned, as though he wasn't sure whether or not to believe her. "What about him?"

Rina shook her head. "I can't trust him. I can't fully love anyone I don't trust, and I can't rule by the side of someone who would betray me."

"So this is about your kingdom."

"No, Troy, this is about you. You and me. I love you."

His face broke into a smile. "Yes. I'll marry you."

"Now?"

Troy pulled her close. "Oh, Rina, are you sure this is what you want?"

"I've never been more sure of anything. The cleric from the East Village is in the camp. I don't want anything else to come between us."

Troy laughed. "You know I would do anything for you. Let's get married."

Rina hurried from the tent and found the cleric. "Troy and I would like to be married. Right away, before we go to war. Will you perform the rites?"

The cleric agreed, and Rina called her people together. "Very soon, we will be at war with the king. But I want to remind you all why we're doing this. We're doing it for our families, for our livelihoods. We will create a land where our children have enough to eat. Where we can come and go as we please, without fear of sorcerers or monsters. We will grow old and die, and we will produce new life."

She looked around, allowing her happiness to shine through the smile on her face. "And we will marry. More specifically, I am going to marry Troy. I would like to invite you all to join with us in our celebration."

Rina and Troy stood before the cleric and repeated his words, to love, honor, and cherish one another, to rule together in peace and justice.

The cleric took their two hands, clasped together, in his, and raised them up. "I present to you Her Majesty, Queen Rina of

Legerdemain, and His Majesty, King Troy of Legerdemain. May their reign be prosperous and peaceful."

Parley

"They're coming." The sentry bowed before Rina, panting.

"Thank you." Rina walked into the clearing. She wore her finest dress, dusty from being stored in a trunk but still elaborate enough to turn heads.

A moment later, Troy stepped into the clearing, followed by Jarok and four of the highest-ranking sorcerers, a woman and three men, who served the king.

Jarok's eyes sparked with longing for one instant before his features hardened. "You betrayed me."

"I was never loyal to you."

"Really? Everything," his voice was heavily weighted with insinuation, "was a lie? You were nothing more than a spy the whole time?"

"Of course not. I had no idea who you were when we met."

"And…after?"

Heat rose to her cheeks. "It was only after I learned of your loyalty to William and your complicity in destroying this land and its people that I turned against you."

"What do you mean complicity? Who have I destroyed?"

"You killed my mother."

Jarok's face fell. "I am the king's head sorcerer. I must follow his orders. Despite everything, I must be loyal to him."

"That is why I asked you to come. I represent the True Heir to the throne. William will fall, of that there is no doubt. I give you one chance to switch your loyalties to the True Heir. Join us, or you will be overthrown with the king."

Jarok's lips tightened in a firm line. "I can't."

"Then you have sealed your own fate."

124

"No, you don't understand. I *can't*. I am tied to the king by blood. My power and the power of his reign are tied together. I cannot break free from him. I *must* obey his will."

He turned to the other sorcerers. "You are free to choose your own way. I will not stop you or betray you to the king."

One woman stepped forward and bowed before Rina. "I want no part of this fight. I came to this land on the promise that I could use magic freely and be compensated richly. I've no wish to be part of a civil war, but the king would not let me leave. If you will grant me safe passage through the woods, I will leave the king's service and not threaten you."

Rina nodded. "Agreed."

The two men bringing up the rear whispered to one another while the third man stepped forward. "I have no love for this king or his ways. I would fight alongside you for the sake of the True Heir if you will have me."

Rina nodded. "What is your name, sir?"

"I am called Menden, my lady."

"Be welcome, Menden." Rina looked at the others. "Have you made a decision?"

"I would like to go with the lady and leave this province," one said. "This is not my war."

"So be it. And you?" She asked the final sorcerer.

"I serve the king and my Lord Sorcerer Jarok. I cannot defect."

"I understand. I will grant you safe passage back out of the forest. After that, this parley ends and we are at war."

"Yes, my lady."

Rina nodded to Troy. He stepped close and leaned in. She spoke softly in his ear. "Escort them along the safe path to the edge of the forest. If they try to turn against you, step off the safe path and let the monsters have them." She touched a vial that hung around his neck.

125

"You have protection. Don't let them hurt you."

Troy beckoned to Jarok and the other. "This way."

As soon as they disappeared, Rina turned to those that remained. "As long as you stay close to me, you'll be safe. I'll escort you to the edge of the forest and then you'll be free."

She started walking, staying far enough from the road that they wouldn't be caught by any of the king's sentries, and staying off the safe trails so they couldn't find their way back once they left.

It was nearing dusk by the time they drew near.

Rina stopped. "Take a rest. We'll be there soon."

One of the magicians who said he wanted to leave took a drink from a water skin and handed it to Rina. "Tell me about the True Heir. How do you know he's the rightful king? Why do you follow him?"

Rina took the skin but didn't drink. "That information is relevant only to the True Heir's followers. Anyone else can learn of it when the True Heir takes the throne and establishes peace with the surrounding countries."

A growl echoed in the forest a few feet away. "We need to move before the monsters decide they're hungry enough to risk getting close." She handed the water skin back to the sorcerer. He grabbed her wrist and pulled her close, pressing a knife to her throat. "Tell me how to find the True Heir or I'll kill you."

Rina laughed. "Fool. The True Heir lives in the center of the forest. You wouldn't survive without me."

The monsters haven't attacked us yet. I don't believe they will."

"You're an idiot." Rina brought her arm up and shoved her elbow into his nose, causing a wave of blood to stream from it. She pushed him, sending him staggering backward. His knife grazed her neck and a trickle of blood slid down.

The sorcerer pulled a charm from his coat and started muttering an incantation.

126

Rina pulled a bag of powder from the pouch on her belt and threw it at him.

He screamed and dropped the charm.

A moment later, a monster crept forward. Its head was like that of a large cat, but its body was covered in scales and it walked on two strong, hind legs while its two front limbs protruded like gangly arms. It padded forward, crouched, then pounced on the bleeding sorcerer.

A second beast, this one akin to a bear with a beak, crashed through the trees from behind them. The sorceress screamed.

Rina wiped the blood from her neck and smeared a streak on Menden, then grabbed the sorceress' hand, smearing blood on her as well. She pulled them both close. "Don't move."

The second monster took a step toward them. The sorceress chanted something. A wave of light streaked toward the creature and seemed to melt into it without effect. It took a step closer, snarling.

Rina stretched her hand, bloody palm out, toward the creature.

It sniffed the blood, growled, then went to join the first monster over the body of the dead sorcerer.

Rina picked up the charm he'd dropped and stuck it in her pouch.

"I would very much like to leave now," the sorceress said.

Rina nodded and led them the rest of the way to the edge of the forest in silence.

When they reached the meadow on the other side of the forest, the sorceress bowed deeply. "Thank you, my lady. I owe you my life." She turned and began the long walk toward the distant lights of a small village.

When she was gone, Menden bowed to the ground. "You are the True Heir. I should've seen before. I pledge to you my fealty and my life. I pledge to you my service as your sorcerer."

Volunteer

Troy watched Rina pace back and forth in their small hut. She was so beautiful, even with her hair in disarray and dried blood streaking her skin.

"I need to get the amulet. It's the source of the king's power. As long as he has it, he cannot be killed."

"I'll get it."

She ignored him. "If I could only get inside the palace. But they've seen me. They know who I am. *He* knows who I am. Without Jarok's invitation, I never would've gotten into the palace in the first place, but especially now—I can't ask him."

"I can get in."

"Don't be absurd, Troy. I won't risk you. Besides, if you get caught, they'll know what we're after, and we'll never have another chance. Maybe I can get one of the servants allied with us to help me." She stared at the roughly drawn map of the palace on the makeshift desk, fully absorbed in her plans.

Troy sighed. She said it was because she couldn't risk him, but he knew what she meant was that she couldn't trust him. She'd never let anyone do anything for her. The notion of destiny seemed to mean she had to do everything herself.

He left the hut. A group of Rina's followers sat around the fire, roasting fresh meat for the rations. "I'm going to go see about getting some supplies," he said. "If Her Majesty asks, I'll be back by evening."

He threw his king's guard cloak over his shoulders and hurried along the safe path out of the forest. Soon, he was out of the comfortable shade and in the blazing heat of the sun, wilting like every plant this side of the forest. He jogged toward the palace, staying hidden as well as he could by the sparse trees and buildings, until he reached the imposing castle wall. Two guards stood by the entrance. One bowed when he saw Troy's cloak.

The other raised an eyebrow, glancing over him suspiciously. "Haven't seen you in a bit. Heard you defected."

"On the contrary, I have valuable information for the king. I infiltrated the True Heir's camp. I have come to warn the king of an imminent attack."

"You stay here," the suspicious one said to the other. He nodded to Troy. "Come on, then." He walked with Troy up the long flights of servants' stairs to the main hall. "Wait here."

He entered the throne room, then returned a few moments later. "The king and his advisor will see you."

Troy entered the throne room and bowed before the king. "Your Majesty, I come with urgent news. I took it upon myself to seek out the True Heir's camp after I learned the general of the rebellious faction is a girl I once knew. I have been successful in my quest to gain her trust. I have just discovered the True Heir has magic that will destroy your power. I came immediately to warn you."

The king turned and looked at his advisor. "Is this possible?"

His advisor, Jarok, eyed Troy with more suspicion than the guard had. "It is true that he is trusted by the enemy. I have seen him with the rebel general. I would've sworn he was loyal to her, however."

Troy fought to keep his demeanor cool.

This man, this aged, disloyal, arrogant bastard was the one Rina had chosen. She'd only come running to Troy's arms after this miserable wretch broke her heart. Jealousy suffused him, making him tremble.

He clenched his fists, bowing his head so Jarok wouldn't see the hate in his eyes. "I had to make her think I was loyal in order to get more information from her. I could not risk her finding out my true agenda, even at the cost of casualties, until the king's own life was threatened. Not long ago, three of your sorcerers defected, did they not?"

129

The king looked livid as he glared at Jarok. "You told me they just wanted to go home."

So, the sorcerer had kept his promise to Rina not to give her away. At least there was that.

"He was right. One of the sorcerers made it through the forest and back to her own land. One was eaten by the forest monsters, and the third sought the True Heir for protection. He is the source of the magic that threatens to destroy you."

"What sort of magic?"

"A curse that will render you powerless, using the very thing you think keeps you safe. An amulet that is bound to you. The sorcerer will use your connection to it to bind you. As long as you are touching it, he will control you."

"Is such a thing possible?" the king demanded.

Jarok looked confused. "Magic draws on connections naturally. It's possible such a connection could be used against you."

"Go get Ada," the king ordered. "Maybe she can foresee a solution."

Jarok bowed and hurried from the room.

The time was now. Troy reached into the satchel under his cloak and drew out a packet of powder. He threw the dust at the king.

The potion was enough to make the king stagger back, coughing and disoriented.

Troy rushed forward and grabbed the chain that hung from the king's neck, yanking the amulet free and stuffing it in his satchel. He dashed from the throne room, through the empty hall, and down the stairs to the courtyard. In a few moments he was at the stable. He pushed past the stable boy and pulled the first horse from his stall, mounted, and thundered from the stable.

He almost ran into an old woman coming into the stable.

The woman gasped, her eyes glazing over and her body

convulsing. Troy didn't wait to see what happened to her. He raced on, toward the gate.

"Stop him!" the old woman yelled.

She was too late. The gate had been opened to let her in and he raced through.

The old woman followed.

Troy sped toward the safety of the forest, but the old woman drew closer.

She chanted some sort of spell, and Troy's horse stumbled, toppling to the ground.

Rolling off, he kept running. Only a few more feet to the safety of the safe path.

The old woman was only inches behind him. She struck him with something. Pain shot through him.

He stumbled on.

Almost there.

He had to get the amulet to Rina.

Like a vision, she stood before him, creeping quietly through the trees.

A few more steps, and…

The old woman's spell struck him again.

He crumbled to his knees and the world went black.

Stolen

Ada steered her horse toward the stable. Herbs were growing fewer within the limits of the kingdom, and she dared not go more than a few steps into the forest. She hated having to rely on the king for favors, but she would have to ask him to replenish her stock when he sent to the other kingdoms for supplies.

She stretched her back. Riding so long pained her more than it used to. As soon as she got inside, she'd order a hot bath. She might even use some of her hoarded herbs to soothe her muscles.

A horse burst from the stable, its rider urging it forward with shouts. His leg brushed hers as he passed.

A vision struck her. She couldn't make out the images directly, but she felt pain and death, all surrounding something that the young man carried on his flight from the castle.

The amulet.

She couldn't say how she knew. It wasn't directly in the vision. But she knew.

And she had to stop him.

She turned her horse and gave chase, racing over the miles of pastureland toward the forest.

Her horse lagged, already weary.

No. She couldn't let him get away. Drawing on the little magic she knew, through the little bit of energy that still swirled in the atmosphere, she touched her horse's flank, giving it new strength and speed.

Little by little, she started to gain on the thief.

Not quickly enough. The forest drew nearer. He would be safe when he reached it.

She urged her horse a little faster. She conjured a spell and hurled it at the young man.

It hit the horse, causing it to stumble, throwing the rider. The rider rolled, then got up and kept running, the horse running right along beside him.

Too late.

He reached the edge of the forest.

Ada threw another spell. This one struck the man in the back, just as he was about to disappear from sight.

Ada dismounted and followed him. She threw another spell.

This one hit its mark. She could feel the life drain from him as he toppled to the ground. Now, to retrieve the amulet.

She paused at the edge of the forest. Magical vibrations quivered around her from every side. The monsters, the relative abundance of energy flowing through the earth, and something else. Something she couldn't quite define, but that was connected to the amulet.

She took a tentative step into the border of the trees and paused, waiting for the monsters to pounce.

Nothing.

She took a step further in.

Still no sign of the monsters. She hobbled forward, shuffling as quickly as she could, forcing her aching limbs to take another step, and another toward where the thief's body lay.

A twig cracked under her foot. She paused, then stepped forward again. She pulled back the hood of her cloak so she could get a better look.

Thunk.

A knife struck a tree, inches from her head. She whimpered and lifted her hands in the air. "Please don't kill me. He stole something from me. Let me take it, and you can have any other valuables you find on him."

A young woman's voice floated out from behind a tree. "Leave this place at once. You may take the horse, but you must go. If you stay, I cannot guarantee your safety."

Ada gave a shaky laugh and took another step forward. "If I do not get back what he stole, I will die anyway."

"What he has is mine."

No. Ada wouldn't let her have it. Perhaps she could convince the woman in another way. She bowed her head. "I can see the future. If you let me leave with what is mine, I will tell your fortune."

She took another step.

The woman threw another knife, this one landing near Ada's feet.

"Please," Ada begged. "My people are in danger. The king is in danger."

"The king is evil. If what's in that bag helps you save him, you give me another reason to stop you."

How could she argue? It was true. But it was only a small part of the truth. "You don't understand. I have seen the future. The one who kills the king will destroy us all."

"Perhaps death is better than life under a king who oppresses his people and forces his magicians to fill the woods with monsters so none can escape his rule."

"You escaped."

"I did. And I will help others, using what is in that bag."

"I cannot let you have it." Ada dropped her arms and made a dash for the body.

The next knife struck her in the chest. She fell backward, gasping for breath.

The young woman emerged from her hiding place. She picked up the satchel and opened it. "With this, I can break the king's protection so he can be killed. Why would you not want me to have it?"

A vision coursed through Ada. The same, yet more terrifying

than anything she'd yet seen. "It's you," she rasped. "You're the one who will kill us all."

War

Rina sat in her little hut, hugging her knees to her chest, tears streaming down her face.

If only she'd gotten to him sooner. She'd seen his body in the middle of the safe path, a horse nearby, and known he couldn't have been there long.

Then she saw the satchel still draped over his shoulder.

Why did he go after the amulet, when she'd expressly told him not to?

She hadn't had time to grieve. Whoever had killed him would be looking for the amulet, and she had to get it first. His death would not be in vain.

The old woman surprised her. She'd expected a soldier at least, possibly a sorcerer, but it was a diminutive crone who stepped from the cover of the trees.

A sorceress, perhaps, with her claims of knowledge about the future, but Rina had killed plenty of sorcerers. This one was no different. A knife to her chest sent her to the ground.

Rina ignored her dire predictions as she retrieved the amulet from Troy's satchel.

"Oh, Troy," she murmured. "I told you not to. I would've figured something out."

She clutched the amulet in her hand, the edges digging into her palm.

"My Lady?" a timid voice at the entrance of her hut said. "They found his body."

"I'll be out in a moment."

She dried her face with a cloth and smoothed her hair. Her people needed to see her as a queen, not as a lovesick peasant. Lifting her head, she strode from her hut to where her men had set Troy's body. She traced the lines of his face with her fingertips. So strong, so kind. Through everything, even her liaison with Jarok, he'd been her support, her strength, the truest friend and gentlest lover she could ask for.

She looked at her followers, turning a slow circle to rest her gaze on each of them.

She raised her arm, holding the amulet above her head. Blood seeped out where the edges had cut her skin. "Troy died to bring me this. This is the key to overthrowing the king. It is from this he derives his power, from this he controls his sorcerers. And it is with this that I will destroy him. The time is now. Gather your weapons. In an hour, we will march to the palace."

She turned to Menden. "With me."

She led him into her hut and laid out her stores of plundered magical items. "I need your help. I've learned I'm connected to this amulet through my father, the rightful king. I need to use it to break William's power over the monsters and the sorcerers."

"The sorcerers are very weak. As you know, they've depleted the elements so there isn't much left to draw from. That also means once we leave this forest, I will have limited powers, too."

"You won't need them if you can help me control the monsters."

Menden took the amulet and held it. "I can feel the connection between the amulet and the monsters, but I don't know what I can do to bond them to you. From what I sense, you're already bonded to them. I can make a potion that should make them more pliable."

"Can you make something to free them from the forest?"

He nodded. "I can try."

"Thank you. And I need one more thing. A potion that I can mix with my blood to protect the people from the monsters."

Menden nodded. "That is something I can do. It's mostly a matter of amplifying your blood to make it stretch further. I'll get started

137

right away."

Rina left him to his work and stood next to Troy's body. Around her, people buzzed back and forth, preparing for battle, but she hardly saw them. She took Troy's cold hand in one of hers. The other rested absently against her stomach. "You were a good man, Troy. I'll never forget you."

"My lady," Menden called. "I need a sample of your blood."

Rina drew a knife and sliced a long slash in her arm. Hardly an inch of skin remained without a scar. It was the price she paid to protect her people.

Her blood dripped into the bowl Menden held under her arm. He chanted as he mixed it with the other ingredients, then divided the potion into four jars. "Send four teams to the Villages. Anyone who wishes to follow you must put this somewhere on their skin. It will be absorbed and mix with their blood. That should protect the people from the monsters. The other potion is almost ready."

Rina called eight of her most loyal followers and divided them into pairs, handing each pair a jar of the potion and giving them Menden's instructions. They followed the safe path toward the kingdom.

"A few more minutes and I'll be done," Menden told her.

"Rina nodded. She strapped on her sword and tucked her knives into her sleeves and belt. She stood on a stump at the center of the camp and shouted for all to hear. "Be ready! We're taking back our land!"

Dead by Morning

Ada lay gasping, staring up at the failing light between the leaves of the trees.

Something rustled the bushes nearby. Was it one of the monsters?

Blood crusted around the knife still protruding from her chest. She pulled it out and examined it. The hilt bore the symbol of the royal line. An official knife belonging to one of the king's guards. The boy she'd been following? She thought he looked familiar. He must have given the knife to the girl. And the girl must've trusted him implicitly to send him to get the amulet. And now she had it.

Thunder rumbled overhead. All the omens were coming true.

The bushes rustled again. An ancient spell protected her from much harm, but being torn limb from limb by a magical monster was likely too much to come back from.

Rolling over, she carefully pushed herself to her knees, then stood.

Her horse, as well as the boy's, had wandered off.

Slowly at first, gaining momentum as she willed her legs to move, she made her way back toward the countryside. The beast followed her, leaves crunching underfoot as it stalked her, but it didn't attack. Maybe her magic was good protection against them, after all.

The sky was dark by the time she escaped from the confines of the woods, and by the time she made it back to the palace, it was into the early hours of the morning. Even still, the palace buzzed with activity.

The guard at the door to the throne room nearly fell over in relief when he saw her. "Ada, where have you been? We've been looking everywhere for you. There's trouble."

"I know." She pushed through the door.

The king whirled around when she came in. "The amulet is gone."

"I know."

"What have your omens told you? Can you see what's happening?"

"The amulet has been stolen by the True Heir. The messenger she sent to retrieve it is dead, killed by a spell I cast on him, but she has the amulet."

"She?"

"Yes."

"Who is *she*?"

Ada narrowed her eyes. "She is the True Heir."

The king threw up his hands. "I know what she calls herself, but who *is* she? Where did she come from? Why does she think she can take my kingdom?"

"Isn't it obvious? She thinks she can take the kingdom because she *can*."

"The amulet is tied to me. My blood. It has no more power for her than any other peasant."

Ada closed her eyes, remembering that night long ago. She hadn't believed it could be true, hadn't understood until that moment in the woods when she lay on the forest floor, a dagger in her chest, and the eyes of the dead queen stared down at her. "Think, William. This girl survives in the forest, thriving amidst monsters of your creation that only you are immune to. She calls herself the True Heir. She claims royal blood and the right to the throne, and she will use the amulet to claim her birthright."

The king's face went pale. "It isn't possible. The baby was a boy and I killed him."

"Yes. But that night, the queen gave birth to twins. The firstborn, a baby girl, was smuggled out of the palace by a servant, raised by a

140

peasant. The True Heir is your niece, the daughter of King Maury. And now she will take her throne by force."

"What can we do? How can we stop her?"

Ada laughed, a dry, bitter cough. "We can't stop her. I have seen what she will do. A storm is coming, lightning that will set fire to the villages, earthquakes that will shake the land, rain that will burn anyone it touches. We'll be lucky if we're not all dead by morning."

The End, Part One

Rina stood at the edge of the forest and sprinkled the potion along the tree line, then on the amulet. She spoke the words Menden had given her. The gem in the center of the amulet glowed, soft purple light casting a gleam in front of her. The glow brightened, making the air around her shimmer.

The aura grew, stretching like a bubble, covering her and expanding over the trees around her until it broke with a loud crack. The light dimmed to a pale glow, softly pulsing in her hand, like the heartbeat of the monsters she could now feel connected to her through the amulet. They were coming toward her, dozens of them, obeying the silent call of the amulet.

She marched along the road, followed by her army, toward the palace and the king.

The monsters drew closer; she could feel their presence, marching behind her, emerging from the trees as though they'd never been imprisoned there, along the long, dark road through the South Village and on toward the castle at the center of the kingdom.

Dawn broke over the trees to her right, casting long, lean shadows on the barren ground beside her, stretching out as she approached the palace walls.

As they drew close, the castle gates opened and the king's guards swarmed out. From high on the walls, the king's voice, magnified through the use of magic, rang out over her. "Surrender, or you'll all be killed."

Rina beckoned to Menden. "Can you make my voice do that?"

Menden nodded and pulled a charm from his pouch.

Rina spoke to the king's soldiers. "I am the True Heir, the daughter of the rightful king, Maury. I have come to claim my throne.

142

Choose your loyalty."

The castle gate opened just enough to let an old lady out. She leaned heavily on a cane and hobbled through the ranks of soldiers that guarded the gate, coming to stand before Rina.

"You," Rina gasped. "I thought—"

"It takes more than a knife to the chest to kill me, girl. I am here to warn you. I have seen the future. You will destroy everyone if you use that." The old woman pointed to the amulet.

"I have to use it. It is the only way to destroy William."

"If you destroy William, you'll destroy everyone and everything in this land."

"I cannot retreat. William has already destroyed this land. The people are dying. His magicians have raped the land until it can no longer support us, yet no one can leave because he has trapped them here. And it doesn't stop with our borders. He plans to expand his reach until he has destroyed the whole world. It is my destiny to stop him."

"Please hear me. If you use the amulet, fire and burning rain will pour from the sky. You'll destroy more than William has."

"I'm sorry. It is a risk I must take."

Rina drew her knife and sliced a gash in her arm, across the lines of other cuts, and let the blood drip onto the amulet. She raised it into the air above her head and yelled the incantation. She hung the amulet around her neck, but still held it, purple gem facing out.

The earth began to tremble, the whole ground shaking as dozens of monsters ripped through the ranks toward the king's soldiers.

Rina's men, protected by the potion of her blood, were ignored, while the king's soldiers were torn apart.

Rina stepped forward, past the old woman who huddled next to the palace wall weeping, and up to the gate. She aimed the light of the amulet at the gate.

It crumbled, disintegrating before her.

Explosions of fire rained down on Rina's monsters and men from the ramparts above. The sorcerers had joined the fight.

Rina could feel the strength draining from the amulet as the magic was used up. She had to kill the sorcerers.

She ran up the stairs along the inside of the outer wall. One of the sorcerers saw her and aimed a fireball her direction. She raised the amulet to block it. The amulet absorbed the spell and spit it back out, directly at the sorcerer.

He disintegrated like the gate below.

One by one, with the light from the amulet, Rina killed the sorcerers that lined the wall.

The sky darkened, heavy storm clouds rolling in. Below, the king's army had been decimated by the monsters.

Instead of satisfying them, however, each kill only seemed to increase their bloodlust. They were now turning on Rina's army, screaming in pain from the protection spell, but killing anyway.

What had she done?

The End, Part Two

Rina aimed the light of the amulet at one of the monsters.
Nothing.

She looked for the old woman. Where had she gone? She was no longer by the gate.

Purple lightning flashed from the sky, striking the villages and fields, igniting them with unearthly fire.

People streamed from the buildings, scattering in all directions. A few of the monsters turned from the carnage of the battle. They raced toward the fleeing villagers, fangs bared.

No. No, this wasn't supposed to happen.

Rina stared at the amulet in her hand.

How could she stop it? How could she end this?

She had to find the king. He created the monsters. He was connected to the amulet. Maybe killing him would stop it.

It was her only chance.

She made her way to the throne room. The king sat on his throne, sipping a glass of wine as though no battle raged outside.

Beside him stood Jarok.

Her heart skipped at the sight of him. She still felt the magnetic pull of him, luring her, teasing her with its force. In the pit of her stomach, something fluttered, a visceral response to his nearness.

She shoved the feeling aside and focused on the king, aiming the light of the amulet at him.

Nothing happened.

The king laughed. "You cannot kill me with my own magic, child." He nodded to Jarok. "Kill her."

Jarok stepped forward. His eyes clouded with pain, frustration etched across his handsome features.

He drew his sword and stepped toward her. "I'm sorry."

Rina dropped her hands. She stood still, letting him advance, gazing into his eyes. He leveled the sword at her.

She put a hand on her stomach. "If you kill me, you kill your child."

Jarok stopped. "My what?"

His distraction was enough for her to slide a knife from her sleeve and throw.

It struck him directly in the heart. His eyes widened as he fell to his knees, his sword clattering to the marble floor.

Blood pooled beneath him. The gaps between the marble tiles on the floor ran red.

Rina stepped toward him, brushing her fingers against his face.

He looked up at her, his eyes a mixture of love and hurt.

"Goodbye," she whispered.

Picking up his sword, she advanced toward the king.

He still wore an over-confident smirk. "Gentlemen!"

From behind the tapestries that lined the walls, more than twenty sorcerers emerged. All at once, they began casting spells.

Holding the amulet, Rina dropped to her knees, raising her hand above her head. The amulet absorbed the spells, shooting sparks back in all directions.

The king took on a horrified expression as his sorcerers ceased to exist before his eyes. When they were all dead, Rina stood and advanced once more, sword in hand.

The king faced her and drew his own sword. Metal clashed with metal, the ringing echoing through the room as they danced around each other.

The door banged open. The old woman stood there, drenched in rain. "Stop!"

Rina paused.

The king took the advantage and slashed with his sword, slicing a gash across Rina's chest.

Gasping from the pain, Rina lashed out at him, jabbing his shoulder. Blood poured from the wound, staining the king's cloak.

"You must break his connection to the amulet," the old woman said.

Rina parried the king's blow.

"His blood. You're both connected to it by blood. You need his blood to break it."

Rina lunged forward, the amulet in hand.

The king's sword pierced her shoulder, running straight through, but she didn't stop. She pushed against him, shoving the amulet against the wound in his shoulder.

The king screamed as the amulet seemed to draw his life into itself.

A moment later, he fell to the ground, vacant, lifeless eyes staring at the ceiling.

Rina pulled his sword from her side and slumped to the ground, weakly trying to put pressure on the wound.

The old woman hurried to her side. "You can't stop yet. The monsters are still out there. The connection to the king is broken, so they're mortal now, but they're still alive, killing your people. Your Majesty." The old woman rubbed a salve into Rina's wounds and wrapped a cloth bandage around her. "Go quickly."

"Why are you helping me?"

"Because it's too late to stop you, and you're the only chance at stopping complete devastation."

"Thank you." Rina forced herself to her feet. The salve in her wounds burned, but somehow it felt good. Restorative.

She limped the first few steps, but picked up speed as the salve coursed through her body. She hurried outside and back up to the top of the wall.

Purple lightning still flashed from the sky.

Using Menden's charm, she amplified her voice. "The king is dead. The monsters are mortal. Get the people to safety and kill the creatures."

She flashed the amulet at a beast that gnawed on a soldier's arm. It evaporated in a hiss of purple steam.

Her soldiers began slashing at the beasts with their swords, wounding and killing them.

A drop of rain splattered on Rina's arm, burning her skin. Another drop fell, and another, hissing and sizzling as they struck, burning through the dusty ground.

"Find shelter! Anything you can, and get as many people to safety as possible."

Her soldiers as well as the soldiers of the king gathered people into the castle. The wounded and those who were too slow to make it inside screamed in agony as the rain burned their flesh.

Lightning lanced the sky, striking trees and buildings. From her perch, Rina could see the Four Villages, one in each direction, begin to blaze as thatch roofs were struck. She couldn't tell from that distance, but she could imagine the villagers running from their burning homes only to be seared by the rain. She prayed they would find other shelter and be safe.

Beside her, the old woman moaned softly. "And so it ends."

Rina shook her head. "This is not the end. Only the pain of a new beginning."

Three Months Later

Rina stood on the parapet overlooking her country. The gems in the crown she wore caught the light from the setting sun, sending prisms dancing on the stone wall. Blades of new grass covered the countryside in a brilliant green blanket.

Those who had survived the monsters, the lightning, and the acidic rain worked steadily to rebuild the villages, singing despite their losses from the hope that grew with the crops. A few monsters had escaped and still roamed the woods, but they could be killed now. All but a few of the king's sorcerers were dead or returned to their own lands. Trade had resumed, and the people were content.

Rina absently rubbed her stomach.

"It's a boy, if I'm reading the omens correctly."

Rina jumped. How did someone Ada's age sneak about so?

"His name will be Troy. For his father, my husband and my most trusted general."

A frown creased Ada's brow. "Are you certain of that?"

"No. But it will be all he ever knows."

Dear Reader,

Thank you for reading *The Heir*. This story began as a collection of short stories that I published on the blog I write for, New Authors Fellowhip (newauthors.wordpress.com). I had no idea when I first wrote *Rendezvous* that I would grow to love this world so much and that the story would grow into what it is today.

Now that I've been immersed in this world, I have so many plans for the other stories that will exist in The Amulet Saga. I hope you'll join me for the journey.

If you enjoyed this story, please tell a friend. Better yet, buy them their own copy.
You can find the rest of The Amulet Saga on Amazon:

The Defector
The Silver Shores
The Prophecy
The Sorceress
The Beginning
The End

Other Books by Avily Jerome:

The Breeding

I love connecting with readers. Please find me on my website (www.avilyjerome.com) or on Facebook (https://www.facebook.com/AvilyJ?fref=ts).

About the Author

Avily Jerome is a writer and freelance editor. She spent five years as the Editor of *Havok Magazine*. Her short stories have been published in multiple magazines, both print and digital. She has judged several writing contests, both for short stories and novels, and she is a book reviewer for Lorehaven Magazine.

She loves all things SpecFic and writes across multiple genres. She is also a writing conference teacher and presenter, and she enjoys speaking to local writers' groups and going to SFF cons.

She is a wife and the mom of five kids. She loves living in the desert in Phoenix, AZ, and when she's not writing, she loves reading, spending time with friends, and experimenting with different art forms.

You can find her on her social media and on her website, at www.avilyjerome.com

www.ingramcontent.com/pod-product-compliance
Lightning Source LLC
Chambersburg PA
CBHW071920220626
47052CB00002B/430